"So all those tabloid stories about you dating various Hollywood starlets are lies?"

"There's only one woman I'm feeling right now. She's a tenacious TV newscaster with beautiful eyes and a gorgeous smile, but unfortunately she thinks I'm a complete jerk." Demetri bent his head low and dropped his mouth to her ear. "Don't know if I can change her perception of me, but I'm going to try. Starting right now..."

Then Demetri covered her mouth with his lips.

Stunned, Angela felt her eyes widen and her breath catch in her throat. She couldn't describe the feelings that washed over her when their lips touched. The urgency, the hunger and the passion of his kiss overwhelmed her. His caress was tender, his hands soft and his lips the best thing she'd ever had the pleasure of tasting. Using his tongue, he parted her lips and eagerly explored every inch of her mouth.

Books by Pamela Yaye

Harlequin Kimani Romance

Other People's Business
The Trouble with Luv'
Her Kind of Man
Love T.K.O.
Games of the Heart
Love on the Rocks
Pleasure for Two
Promises We Make
Escape to Paradise
Evidence of Desire
Passion by the Book
Designed by Desire
Seduced by the Playboy

PAMELA YAYE

has a bachelor's degree in Christian education. Her love for African-American fiction prompted her to pursue a career in writing romance. When she's not working on her latest novel, this busy wife, mother and teacher is watching basketball, cooking or planning her next vacation. Pamela lives in Alberta, Canada, with her gorgeous husband and adorable but mischievous son and daughter.

Seduced
BY THE PLAYBOY

Pamela Yaye

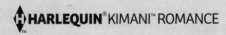

HARLEQUIN® KIMANI™ ROMANCE

Recycling programs
for this product may
not exist in your area.

ISBN-13: 978-0-373-86361-7

SEDUCED BY THE PLAYBOY

Copyright © 2014 by Pamela Sadadi

For questions and comments about the quality of this book please contact us at CustomerService@Harlequin.com.

Printed in U.S.A.

™ www.Harlequin.com

Dear Reader,

I've had the Morretti brothers—Demetri, Nicco and Rafael—in my mind for years (don't tell my husband!), so I'm thrilled about Seduced by the Playboy, the first book in the Morretti Millionaires series. Their parents, Arturo and Vivica Morretti, are a dynamic couple who've raised three successful, drop-dead sexy sons oozing with charm, charisma and killer swag. I look forward to you meeting the Morretti brothers and the women who fall head over heels for them.

The youngest of the brood, Demetri Morretti, is every woman's dream, but Angela Kelly's worst nightmare. When the baseball superstar and the tenacious news reporter meet, sparks fly, but after their explosive argument at WJN-TV goes viral, Angela is more determined than ever to keep her distance from the surly baseball player with the massive ego. Unfortunately, Demetri has other plans!

Nicco Morretti, one of Demetri's brothers, makes a cameo in this book, and once I "met" the famed restaurateur at the grand opening of his restaurant, Dolce Vita Chicago, I knew I had to write his story next. I love watching strong, independent women tame bad boys, and I have a feeling you will, too. Look for Seduced by the CEO next month.

I LOVE, LOVE, LOVE to hear from readers, so drop me a line at pamelayaye@aol.com, find me on Facebook or visit my website, www.pamelayaye.com. Thanks for the support. Happy reading, and be blessed.

With love,

Pamela Yaye

Odidison and Yaye Family: I love you more than anything in the world, and I feel incredibly blessed to have all of you in my life. Thank you for your unconditional love and support.

Sha-Shana Crichton: Can you believe *Seduced by the Playboy* is our fifteenth Harlequin Kimani Romance novel? Thanks for believing in me and my gift when no else did. You are the BEST agent a girl could ask for, and I predict even greater things in our future.

Shannon Criss: I appreciate all of the hard work you've done on the Morretti Millionaires series. Thanks for getting behind this project and for giving me the creative freedom to write the family miniseries of my dreams! :)

The Harlequin Kimani Marketing Team: You guys rock! You create the best book covers in the business, and I couldn't be happier with the Morretti Millionaires series. Keep up the good work!!!

Chapter 1

Demetri Morretti yanked open the door of the sleek, ultra-modern WJN-TV building and stalked inside the bright, bustling lobby. The station was abuzz with activity, the mood was cheerful, and everywhere Demetri turned were young, well-dressed people. Some were drinking coffee in the waiting area, others were yakking into their cell phones, and a few were snapping pictures in front of the life-size bronze statue.

Keeping his head down, and his pace brisk, he strode past the reception desk like a man on a mission. And he was. He'd driven across town to issue a warning to Angela Kelly, the female broadcaster with the lying lips, and wasn't going to let anything stop him. His left shoulder was killing him, throbbing in pain from his neck to his elbow, but he kept his smile in place as he continued through the sun-drenched lobby.

Demetri was about to breeze past the security desk but saw the robust-looking security guard eyeing him and thought better of it.

As he approached the circular desk, he caught sight of the gigantic oak clock. Demetri was surprised to see that it was already eleven-thirty. He was supposed to be meeting his team of his agent, his manager and his no-nonsense publicist for lunch at their favorite uptown pub. But when he remembered last night's episode of *Eye on Chicago,* Demetri decided nothing was more important than confronting the broadcaster who'd slaughtered his name on national television. This was the second time Angela Kelly had taken a cheap shot at him, and he was sick of being the butt of her jokes. This was a detour he had to make— one his manager couldn't talk him out of no matter how hard he'd tried.

"Hey, man, what's up?" Demetri said, greeting the guard with a flick of his head. "I'm here to see Ms. Angela Kelly."

"Now's not a good time."

"This won't take long. I just need a few minutes."

"Do you have an appointment?"

Demetri shook his head. "No, but—"

"But nothing." The guard waved him off with his beefy hand. "Come back at the end of the day. I might be able to squeeze you in then."

"I can't. I'm busy."

"Doing what? Panhandling?"

Taken aback by his comment, Demetri glanced down and inspected his attire. He'd left the house without shaving and wore dark, stubbly hair on his chin, but he didn't look *that* bad, did he? He'd showered and wore his new signature Gucci cologne, and his black Nike warm-up suit didn't have a wrinkle in sight. *I look good,* he decided, squaring his shoulders. *This dude needs to have his eyes checked.*

"You cats from the Ninth Street homeless shelter are driving me nuts," the guard complained. "You're always coming in here begging to see Ms. Kelly just because she volunteers down at the center, but enough is enough. She's too nice to tell you bums to get lost, but I'm not, so get lost!"

Demetri raised his eyebrows for two reasons. One because the security guard thought he was down on his luck, and two because the man spoke about Angela Kelly in glowing terms, as if she were a saint. Demetri found it hard to believe that the mean-spirited newscaster volunteered with the homeless. It had to be a front. Something she did to look good, to boost the ratings of her TV show. Demetri considered leaving, and tracking her down at the shelter up the block, but quickly decided against it. He was going to talk to Angela Kelly today, and the gruff security guard with the unibrow was going to lead him straight to her.

"I'd appreciate if you could help me out," Demetri said, glancing around the lobby for any signs of the enemy. "It's important that I talk to Ms. Kelly *before* she goes on the air."

"Are you deaf? I said to come back later." Glowering, he bared his crooked, coffee-stained teeth. "Scram before I toss you out myself."

Demetri took off his dark aviator sunglasses and flashed his trademark grin. The one that had landed him a seven-figure deal with Sony, Crest toothpaste and a dozen other multimillion-dollar companies. "Now, is that any way to talk to the Athlete of the Year?"

The guard's eyes flew out of his head. "Holy crap! You're Demetri Morretti!"

Leaning forward, Demetri pressed a finger to his lips and spoke in a conspiratorial whisper. "Keep it down, man. I don't want anyone to know it's me."

The guard raced around his desk, cap in hand, a giddy expression on his wide face. "I've been a fan ever since you signed with the Chicago Royals, and I haven't missed a home game since!"

Demetri nodded. "Thanks, man. I really appreciate the support."

"My friends are going to trip when I tell them I met you! We watch your games every week and even drove a thousand miles to see you play in…"

Demetri stood patiently, waiting for the guard to quit rambling about last year's All-Star Game. Unfortunately, this happened several times a day. And although he was out for the rest of the season due to his bum shoulder, there were fans out there who still treated him like a champion. Everyone else had turned on him, and the last thing Demetri needed was more bad press. That was the main reason he'd come to tell Angela Kelly to back off and stop the station from airing the last installment of her *Athletes Behaving Badly* series.

"Can I have your autograph?" the guard asked, snatching a piece of paper off the desk and shoving it under his nose. "No, no, forget that. Can I take a picture with you?"

"I don't know. That depends on whether or not you're going to take me to Ms. Kelly."

"Anything for you, Mr. Morretti. Right this way."

Grinning from ear to ear, he hustled Demetri through the lobby, past the reception desk and down a long, narrow corridor. The scent of freshly brewed coffee filled the air. Offices and conference rooms were on either side of the hallway, and Demetri could hear conversation, laughter and the distant sound of the radio.

The guard stopped in front of a door with the letter *A* marked on it. "This is where Ms. Kelly tapes *Eye on Chicago.*" He wore an apologetic smile. "Sorry, Mr. Morretti, but I'm going to have to ask you to switch off your cell phone before we head inside. I know it's a pain, but those are the rules."

"I figured as much, so I left my cell in the car." Demetri slid his hands into his sweatpants. That wasn't the only reason. His phone had been ringing off the hook ever since he signed his contract extension last week, and he was sick of the incessant calls from his relatives. Everyone needed money for something—to pay his or her mortgage, for tuition, to get a second boob job. If not for his mother's heartfelt pleas, he would have cut his mooching family members off a long time ago.

A siren blared behind him, and his burly escort cursed under his breath.

"I can't believe that stupid alarm is going off again," he grumbled, whipping his walkie-talkie out of his pocket and rattling off a series of security codes. "I'll be right back, Mr. Morretti. Hang tight."

"Take as long as you need, man. I'm not going anywhere."

The security guard took off down the hall, mumbling to himself in Portuguese. Demetri waited until his escort disappeared around the corner, then calmly opened the door of Studio A. People in headsets, clutching wooden clipboards, rushed around the room. He slipped inside the darkened studio with the stealth of a burglar.

The studio was spacious, and the air was thick and hot. He heard a woman speaking and instantly recognized the low, sultry voice. It was the same voice he'd heard in his dreams. The one that had teased and tormented him last night.

After watching *Eye on Chicago* the previous night, and seeing his past transgressions in high definition, he'd stormed into his home gym, fuming mad. But it didn't matter how many push-ups he did or how much weight he lifted because he still couldn't get Angela Kelly's voice out of his head. Or her blistering jabs. *Demetri Morretti is an overrated, overpaid athlete with no class... His off-field behavior has not only disgraced the Chicago Royals organization, but his teammates and fans... If I was the league commissioner, I'd give Morretti the boot, once and for all.*

Demetri clenched his hands into fists. He wanted to punch something, wanted to unleash the anger shooting through his veins. Another workout was definitely in order. He was tense, more fired up than a boxer on fight day, and those deep breathing exercises his conditioning coach had taught him weren't working. They never worked. These days, he was more stressed than ever, and getting injured during the preseason had only made matters worse.

Now stepping out from behind the curtain shielding him, Demetri slid up against the back wall. Standing perfectly still, he zeroed in on the raised stage. Seated behind the V-shaped glass desk was the studio's most popular broadcaster—Angela Kelly. The stunning twentysomething Chicago native with the girl-next-door appeal. Her beauty was jaw-dropping, as breathtaking as a Mediterranean sunset, and at the sight of her dazzling smile his mouth went bone-dry. Everything about her was chic and sophisticated. Her fuchsia blazer and shorts, her silky black hair, the way she spoke and moved. Angela Kelly looked well put together, as if she'd just stepped out of hair and makeup, and she spoke with such exuberance that the entire studio was filled with her positive energy.

And Demetri Morretti hated her on sight.

"Thanks for watching this week's edition of *Eye on Chicago*," Angela Kelly said, staring straight into the camera and wearing her brightest smile. "Make sure you tune in next week for the conclusion of my *Athletes Behaving Badly* story. Until next time, stay safe."

"That's a wrap, people!" the cameraman yelled. "Great job, Angela. You really outdid yourself this week. Faking tears as you read the intro was a nice touch."

"I wasn't faking," Angela said, unclipping her microphone and resting it on the desk. "Watching those clips of teenagers rifling through the garbage was heartbreaking."

"Sure it was." The cameraman winked and then patted her on the back. "I'll see you on Friday. We're filming two segments back-to-back, so make sure you bring your A game."

"I'll bring mine if you bring yours!"

The cameraman chuckled and then strode off the soundstage.

Angela slid off her chair, adjusted her blazer and ran a hand through her perfectly flat-ironed hair. Spotting her boss, Salem Velasquez, at the back of the room, she swiped her clipboard off the raised glass desk and stepped off the set. This was her chance to talk to Salem—alone—about the proposal she'd submitted last week for her new three-part series. Angela was determined to win her boss over. If she wanted to be taken seriously in the journalism community, she had to continue pursuing meatier news stories. Stories that would impact the world and change lives. Stories that she could be proud of. After eight years of covering celebrity gossip, Angela was ready for a change. She was ready for the big leagues. And if she wanted to be the station's lead broadcaster by the time she turned thirty at the end of the year, she had to start pushing the envelope.

"Angela-wouldn't-know-the-truth-if-it-slapped-her-in-the-face-Kelly," a male voice said from behind her. A tall, hooded figure, decked out in all black, slid in front of her.

Angela stepped back with a yelp. "What the hell?" she snapped, touching a hand to her chest. Narrowing her eyes, she studied the lean, muscled stranger. His baseball cap was pulled low, past his eyebrows, a thick Nike hoodie covering his head, and his hands were tucked in the pockets of his sweatpants. His head was down, and his shoulders were bent. The man looked sinister, like the villain in a comic book, but he smelled heavenly.

"I need to have a word with you."

"I'm sorry, but I'm going to have to ask you to leave. This is a closed set, and no one…" Angela's voice faded when the stranger took off his hoodie. Her clipboard slipped out of her hands, falling to the floor with a clatter.

"I'd say it was a pleasure to meet you, but I'd be lying, and I'd hate to make a second trip to confession this week."

Angela felt her eyes widen and her knees buckle. Not because she was surprised by the dig, but because Demetri Morretti—the reigning bad boy of Major League Baseball—was standing in front of her, live and in the flesh.

Her thoughts were running wild, but her gaze was glued to his handsome, chiseled face before her. Dark eyebrows framed his brown eyes, a thin mustache lined his thick lips, and his wide shoulders made him seem imposing, larger-than-life. The half Italian, half African-American star athlete was a force to be reckoned with on the baseball field. And even though he was casually dressed in workout clothes and had a very present five-o'clock shadow, he was still smokin' hot.

His skin was a warm caramel shade of brown and so smooth and flawless-looking, Angela suspected he had weekly facials. Demetri Morretti was a pretty boy if she'd ever seen one, but she didn't think for a second that he was soft. Angela had read enough about the thirty-two-year-old superstar to know that he was a spoiled, ridiculously rich athlete who pushed around anyone who got in his way.

Recovering from the shock of seeing Demetri Morretti in her studio, Angela hit him with an icy glare. "Tapings aren't open to the public," she said tightly. "And since you're not an employee of the station, I'm going to have to ask you to leave, Mr. Morretti."

"I will, as soon as you go on the air and issue an apology to me and my family."

Angela almost laughed in his face but caught herself before a snicker escaped her mouth. No use antagonizing him. According to published reports, Demetri was impulsive, a hothead of the worst kind, and there was no telling what he'd do in the heat of the moment.

"My mother is very upset about the lies you told about me on your show, but I assured her you'd apologize once you realized the errors of your ways."

"Apologize for what? Speaking the truth?" Angela rolled her eyes to the ceiling. She didn't tell Demetri about the countless hours she'd spent reading articles and sports blogs about his background and twelve-year baseball career. The headlines about the gifted shortstop were damning and more salacious than a CIA prostitution scandal. There were reports of bar brawls, drunken Las Vegas parties and explosive run-ins with rival baseball fans. She'd found so much "dirt" on Demetri Morretti, and the other players featured in her story, she'd had enough material for a three-part series. And the viewers were eating it up. Her show had slayed the competition in the ratings last week, and everywhere she went people were talking about her *Athletes Behaving Badly* story. It was a hot topic, one that viewers couldn't seem to get enough of.

"Don't mess with me, Ms. Kelly, because when it's all said and done, I *will* get my way."

Angela's toes curled in her five-inch black pumps. She couldn't believe his nerve. Demetri was rotten to the core, a man of such extraordinary arrogance, Angela didn't know why she was even talking to him. "You might be able to throw your weight around the clubhouse," she began, meeting his hostile gaze, "but it's not going to work here. I double-checked the facts and have taped interviews with eyewitnesses to back up my report."

"Your report was full of lies. It was nothing more than a smear campaign done by a bitter, angry woman who got dissed and dismissed by her ex-boyfriend."

Angela's breath caught in her throat. Her face must have registered surprise, because a grin that could scare a mobster broke out across Demetri's lips.

"Your ex plays for the L.A. Jaguars," he continued. "And he was nice enough to share all of the dirty details of your relationship with him."

Fear blanketed her skin. Licking her dry lips, Angela cast a nervous glance around the studio. She spotted her colleagues at the other end of the room, perusing the snack table, and sighed inwardly. Angela wasn't proud of her past, and the last thing she wanted was for her colleagues to find out about all the wild and crazy things she'd done while living in L.A. It was hard enough being the only woman of color at the TV station, and she didn't want to give the other broadcasters another reason to resent her. Not that they needed one. They thought she was too young to host *Eye on Chicago,* unqualified to work at the station and skating by on her looks. "Who I've dated is none of your business, and furthermore, my personal life has absolutely nothing to do with my *Athletes Behaving Badly* story."

"You see, Ms. Kelly, I did a little digging of my own and discovered that you've dated a lot of professional athletes," he said, stroking his jaw reflectively. "And from what I hear, several of them dogged you out *bad*. That's why you did that story. To get back at the guys who dumped you and to stick it to anyone who plays pro sports."

"That's ludicrous." Lifting her head, Angela arched her shoulders and looked him dead in the eye. She wasn't going to be Demetri Morretti's punching bag. Not now. Not ever. "This conversation is over. Please leave."

"I will, Madame Gold Digger, as soon as you—"

"Gold digger?" Angela repeated, splaying her hands on her hips.

"Did I stutter?"

"I don't know any gold diggers who put themselves through school or who volunteer twenty hours a week at various local shelters, do you?"

Angela saw a bolt of surprise flicker across Demetri's face, but bragging about her volunteer work made her feel small, as if she'd just insulted all of the families she worked with. But her unexpected confession clearly stunned the baseball star, and Angela was determined to use this leverage to her advantage. "I have nothing against you or any of the other athletes mentioned in my story," she said, meaning every word. "I did the piece to warn young women about the perils of pursuing professional athletes and—"

"To stick it to your ex-lovers," he tossed out, mirroring her rigid body stance.

Angela made her eyes thin. "Maybe instead of coming down here and harassing me, you should have gone to the clubhouse to practice."

"What are you trying to say?"

"I saw your last game before your shoulder injury. You jumped every pitch, your timing was way off, and your swing looked lifeless."

Demetri flexed his jaw muscles. He was well aware of his batting slump, and the problems with his swing, but he didn't need anyone—especially a newscaster—reminding him. "There's nothing wrong with my game."

"Oh, but there is. Ask your coach. Ask your teammates. Hell, ask the fans."

"I didn't come down here to get batting tips from a reporter with no conscience," he said, folding his arms. "I came to issue a warning. Go on the air and apologize, or I'll—"

"You'll what?" Angela jeered, cutting him off. "Hurl a beer bottle at me like you did to that poor college kid in Newark? Or get one of your flunkies to rough me up?"

His nostrils flared, and the corners of his lips curled into a scowl. Demetri stepped forward, and when Angela jumped back, she bumped into one of the towering black light stands. A sharp pain stabbed her leg, but it was the menacing gleam in her adversary's eyes that made her knees quiver.

"I'm not going to touch you, Ms. Kelly." Demetri's voice was calm, but his tone was colder than ice. "But if you don't go on the air and apologize, I'll sue you, your boss and this damn station."

Chapter 2

Angela felt a cold chill snake down her back. Swallowing the lump in her throat, she discreetly dried her damp palms along the side of her fitted Chanel shorts. Since part one of her series aired two weeks ago, she'd received scores of hate mail. Several athletes had taken to Twitter to express their anger, but no one had shown up at the station threatening litigation—until now. It wasn't the first time Angela had ruffled someone's feathers, and usually she wouldn't give a threat a second thought. But the way Demetri was staring at her, with his head cocked and his eyes narrowed, made her stomach coil into a suffocating knot.

"So, what's it going to be?" Arms folded, he tapped his foot impatiently on the floor. "Are you going to issue that apology, or are we going to have to hash this thing out in court?".

Angela swallowed hard. Demetri sounded serious, looked serious, too, but she didn't believe him. Not for a second. He was too busy getting into bar fights, throwing wild parties at his Chicago mansion and drag racing in his Maybach to show up in court.

"You're not going to win this, so you might as well give up now."

"Get out," she snapped, pointing at the studio door. "And don't come back!"

"I'll leave, as soon as I get that apology."

Angela glowered but said nothing. What could she say? "Leave or I'll call security"? The baseball star was trespassing, but the security guards weren't going to throw a future hall-of-famer off the property.

"I don't want to play hardball with you, Ms. Kelly, but you leave me no choice. Your report was biased and unfounded. Not to mention full of outright lies."

When Demetri took another step forward, infringing upon her personal space, she imagined herself smacking the broad grin off his face. But instead of acting on her impulse, Angela faked a smile. It was time to try a different approach because arguing with Demetri Morretti was getting her nowhere. "I'll give some thought to what you said, and someone from the station will contact you by the end of the week. Okay?"

Demetri clapped his hands. "Well done, Ms. Kelly. Nicely played. For a second there, I actually believed you were a rational human being."

"Well, at least I'm not a—"

Angela felt a hand on her shoulder and broke off speaking. She turned to her right, and groaned inwardly when she saw her producer, standing beside her, wearing a concerned expression. And worse, everyone in the studio, from the voluptuous makeup artist to the bearded engineer, was now staring at her, with wide eyes and open mouths. How much had her colleagues heard? And why were all of the men in the studio shooting evil daggers at her?

"Welcome to WJN-TV, Mr. Morretti. I'm Salem Velasquez, one of the head producers."

Wearing a tight smile, he nodded and shook the hand she offered.

"If you have a few moments, I'd love to speak to you in private."

"Great. The quicker we resolve this issue the better."

"Please follow me. My office is right this way." Salem motioned to the studio door, and Demetri fell in step beside her.

Angela stayed put. She didn't want any part of this meeting, and she had better things to do than listen to Demetri

Morretti whine about her report. Anxious to return to her office, she turned around and stalked off in the opposite direction. She needed to vent, and her best friend, Simone, was the perfect person to talk to.

"Angela!"

Angela stopped dead in her tracks. Her heart was hammering in her chest. The sharpness of Salem's tone and the booming sound of her voice made Angela break out in a nervous sweat.

Glancing over her shoulder confirmed her worst fears. Now her boss *and* the surly baseball star were glaring at her. The air in the studio was suffocating, so thick with tension, Angela felt as if she was going to faint. And the way Demetri was staring at her—all serious and intense—made her skin prickle with goose bumps.

"You will be joining us."

"Oh, of course," Angela lied, nodding her head. "I was just going to…to…to…"

"Whatever it is can wait. Get in my office. Now."

I'd rather ride a unicycle naked down the Magnificent Mile, she thought, dragging herself across the studio and past her gawking coworkers.

"Please, Mr. Morretti, have a seat," Salem said, gesturing to one of the padded chairs in front of her large oak desk. "Make yourself comfortable."

The small, cramped office was overrun with bookshelves, knickknacks, and the scent of cinnamon was so heavy in the air, Angela's stomach grumbled. It had been hours since she had breakfast, but the thought of eating made her feel queasy. So did the way her boss was smiling at Demetri Morretti. He was the enemy, a man bent on destroying her, and if Salem didn't toughen up and quit making eyes at him, they'd both be out of a job.

"Thanks, but I'd rather stand."

"Very well." Salem sat down in her leather swivel chair and clasped her hands together. "I understand that you're upset about Ms. Kelly's *Athletes Behaving Badly* piece, but I stand behind the story and what was reported. All of our stories are vigorously researched, and we pride ourselves on double-checking every fact and every report."

"No one from your station contacted me or my team."

"I assure you, Mr. Morretti, my assistant phoned your publicist for a statement."

He crossed his arms. "I would like you to provide the name of the person who called and the time and date the call was placed."

Nodding, Salem picked up her pen and made a note on one of the open file folders on her desk. "That's not a problem. I can forward the information to you later today."

Angela raised her eyebrows but didn't speak. She stood at the back of the room, beside the door, and watched the exchange between Salem and Demetri with growing interest. Maybe her boss was going to come through for her after all. Salem's eyes were glued to Demetri's lips, but she sounded confident and looked in control.

"There are two sides to every story, but your report only focused on one side. The side filled with lies. As a result, my character and integrity have been compromised."

What integrity? Angela thought, clamping her lips together to trap a curse inside. *You're a hothead who can't control his temper!* She thought back over every second of her argument with Demetri. And when she got to the point where her boss showed up, Angela decided that was the most humiliating moment of her life. She'd been reprimanded in front of her crew, then ordered into her boss's office to speak to the enemy. Even more troubling, Salem was being nice to him. A little too nice. Her body was angled toward him, and she hadn't stopped smiling since they entered the office. If Angela didn't know better, she'd think Salem had a crush on

Demetri, because the only time she'd ever seen her boss this happy was when she received her annual Christmas bonus.

"If your assistant had contacted me, I would have been here."

"Really?" A quizzical look covered Salem's face. "But it's been widely reported in the media that you don't do interviews."

"You shouldn't believe everything you hear."

Angela wanted to gag. Demetri was lying and making it look easy. He hadn't done an on-camera interview in years, and according to reports, his publicist had to preapprove the questions. The baseball star was a recluse, a man who liked to be alone, who kept to himself. Except when he was getting into bar fights or humiliating waiters and service staff.

Angela looked him over, slowly. Demetri Morretti was a man of great presence, with more natural charisma than an A-list actor. That was probably why people overlooked his bad behavior and made excuses for him. But Angela wasn't one of his crazed fans or easily seduced by ridiculously rich athletes. She decided right then and there that she wasn't going to let Demetri Morretti disrespect her again.

"You seem like a very nice lady, Mrs. Velasquez," Demetri began smoothly, favoring her with a smile that warmed his entire face, "and I don't want to sue you, but if Ms. Kelly doesn't apologize publicly for slandering my name, I will."

Silence filled the air and stretched on for several long minutes.

"I have an idea." Salem's voice was filled with excitement and she practically bounced up and down on her chair. "Why don't you come on *Eye on Chicago* and do an exclusive sit-down interview with Ms. Kelly this month?"

No, no, no! Angela wanted to scream out in protest, but shot evil daggers at Demetri instead. He was bad news, someone she had to stay far, far away from. He was a rich, cocksure athlete who thought he could push her around, and she had absolutely no desire to have him on her show. Not tomorrow. Not next week. Not ever.

"No, thank you. I'm not interested."

"What if we gave you the questions beforehand? You and your team could even add a few of your own. We never do that, but I'm willing to make an exception for you, Mr. Morretti."

"No way!" Angela hollered, the words bursting out of her mouth. "He shouldn't get preferential treatment just because he's a—"

Salem's eyes thinned. In an instant, Angela's jaw locked and her tongue seized up.

"I don't trust reporters." Demetri cast a glance at the back of the room. "Not even the ones who look sweet and innocent. They're the worst kind."

Angela ignored the dig. *Sticks and stones, Morretti. Sticks and stones.* There was nothing the surly baseball player could say to hurt her. Life was good. Great. For the first time ever, her show was on top of the ratings, and next weekend she was covering the grand opening of Dolce Vita.

The posh three-story lounge was the first of its kind in Chicago, and Angela had been looking forward to the event for weeks. Because of her busy schedule, Angela hadn't hung out with her girlfriends in weeks. And since they would be in attendance at the star-studded launch, she was excited about catching up with them and eating some award-winning Italian food.

"If you'll both excuse me," Angela said, gripping the door handle. "I really have to go."

Salem shook her head, and Angela dropped the door handle as if it were a roasted stone. Her boss spoke to Demetri in a soft, soothing voice, but her eyes were glued to Angela. "I want to hear your side of the story, and I bet America does, too."

"I know I don't," Angela grumbled. Her colleagues would

probably jump at the chance to interview Demetri Morretti but the thought of interviewing him, under the bright studio lights, made Angela feel queasy. The camera captured everything—every pause, every nervous glance, every awkward movement—and she feared her nerves would get the best of her and she'd drown on live TV. Add to that the fact that she had to worry about keeping Demetri *and* his ego in check. Angela didn't like him, didn't trust him and had a feeling he was up to no good. He'd embarrassed her once in front of her crew, and there was no doubt in her mind he'd do it again. *What if he outsmarts me on my show?* she thought, swallowing hard. *What if he makes me look like a fool on national television?*

"This would be your opportunity to finally set the record straight," Salem continued. "And imagine what the press could do for you, your team and your charity foundation. It's a win-win situation for everyone involved, and…"

Angela tuned her boss out. Catching sight of her reflection in the wall mirror, she straightened her shoulders and cleaned the scowl off her face. There was nothing she could do about the hatred in her heart, though. Angela was fuming, her pulse pounding violently in her ears.

Her gaze bounced around the room and landed on Demetri. It was easy to see why fans disliked him. Charming one minute, acerbic the next. Former coaches, rivals and the media criticized him for his conduct on and off the field, and after having the misfortune of meeting Demetri for herself, Angela believed the criticism was due. She only wished he wasn't so good-looking. He gave her chills—the ones that started in her toes and shot straight to her core—and it was impossible to ignore his raw masculine energy. Everything about him was a turn-on.

"I'll give it some thought." Demetri took his sunglasses out of his back pocket and slid them on. "My publicist will be in touch."

"That sounds great, Mr. Morretti. I look forward to hearing from her."

"Thanks for your time, Mrs. Velasquez. Have a nice day." Demetri nodded, then turned and strode out of the small, cramped office.

"Angela, I know you're upset because I ordered you into my office, but I had no choice," Salem said, her facial features touched with concern. "You were losing control."

"Of course I was! Demetri Morretti is a complete jerk!" Gesturing to the door, her eyes narrowed and her lips pursed, she raged, "Who the hell does he think he is?"

Salem picked up the latest copy of *People* magazine off her desk and held it in the air. "The sexiest man alive, that's who!"

"I wonder who he had to bribe to get on the cover."

"You're kidding, right?"

"No, Demetri's a jerk, and in my opinion there's nothing sexy about him."

Salem snatched her phone off the cradle and started dialing.

"Who are you calling?" Angela asked, frowning.

"My optometrist." She was wearing a straight face, but her tone was rich with humor. "I'm booking you an emergency appointment."

"Why? My eyes are fine."

"No, they're not." A smirk lit her glossy, pink lips. "There's definitely something wrong with your vision *and* your hormones because Demetri Morretti is the finest man on the planet!"

Chapter 3

The moment Demetri entered MVP Sports Bar & Grill and smelled fresh garlic wafting out of the open kitchen, his mouth began to water. Located a half block from Skyline Field, the sports bar was insanely popular among young and college-aged sports fans. Every time Demetri stopped inside the restaurant bar, the staff gave him a hero's welcome.

"Demetri, my man, so good to see you!" The manager, a portly man with a double chin, grabbed his hand and gave it a hearty squeeze. "How are you doing?"

"Good, Mr. De Rossi. How's the family?"

"My sons are growing up fast and getting in all sorts of trouble." Chuckling, he bent down and pointed at his receding hairline. "The kids are the reason I'm losing my hair, and the little I have left is turning gray!"

Demetri laughed heartily. The fellow reminded him of his dad, right down to his wrinkle-free pants, buffed leather shoes and thick Italian accent. Shooting the breeze with the jovial bar manager always put Demetri in a good mood. And after the tongue-lashing he'd received from Angela Kelly at the station, he needed something to laugh about.

"I just put your calzone in the stove," he said, patting Demetri on the shoulder and steering him toward the dining room. "I'll bring it out as soon as it's ready."

"Thanks, sir. I appreciate it."

Spotting his staff sitting in one of the cushy, padded booths, Demetri acknowledged them with a nod of his head.

Nichola Caruso, his savvy, no-nonsense publicist and personal assistant, waved, but his manager and agent were too busy on their cell phones to notice he'd arrived. Every Friday, he met with his team at MVP Sports Bar & Grill, and because Nichola rented out the entire restaurant, they could eat and talk in peace. Demetri didn't have to worry about paparazzi snapping pictures of him with barbecue sauce on his face or crazed fans hitting him up for autographs or cash. "If it's not too much trouble, can I have a basket or two of bruschetta?" Demetri patted his stomach. "I'm starving, and I bet the guys finished what was on the table."

"No problem. I'll whip up a fresh batch for you."

Demetri thanked him again and strode into the lounge. Dark wood paneling, vintage sports memorabilia and plush burgundy couches created a sophisticated decor. The tall, oversize windows provided a tranquil view of downtown Chicago and plenty of warm sunshine. It was the perfect weather for gardening or reading out on the deck, and as soon as Demetri finished his meeting, that was exactly what he was going to do.

"Sorry I'm late, but the I-94 was backed up for miles," Demetri said, taking off his hoodie and chucking it inside the booth. Sitting down, he snatched a menu off of the table and flipped it open. "Did you guys order already?"

His agent, Todd Nicholas, answered with a nod of his head. Buff, with blue eyes and tanned skin, he looked like the quintessential all-American boy. "I have a meeting across town in an hour, but I couldn't leave here without having Chef Sal's delicious lasagna. I've been craving it all week."

Demetri stared longingly at the barbecue chicken wings and licked his lips.

"Want some?" Nichola picked up the basket and offered it to him. "Go ahead, Demetri. They're all yours."

"Are you sure? I know how much you love Sal's wings."

"I'm sure. I shouldn't be cheating on my diet anyway."

Demetri plucked a wing out of the basket and took a big bite. "Thanks, Nichola. I can always count on you to give me just what I need."

"Just make sure you remember that when my birthday rolls around in August!" she said, swiveling her neck. "I want shopping money *and* Porsche Cayenne in pink just like Mariah Carey!"

Demetri released a hearty chuckle. Small and petite, with a short, funky haircut, Nichola looked more like a high school student than a Princeton graduate. A friend of his family for years, he'd hired her as a favor to his father, Arturo, and in the twelve years Nichola had been working for him, he'd never once regretted his decision.

"You're moving a lot better today." Nichola wore a concerned expression on her face, but her tone was upbeat and bright. "How's the shoulder?"

"Not bad. It's only been a couple weeks since the surgery, but my surgeon and physiotherapist are pleased with my progress."

"Is that where you were this morning? At your doctor's office?"

Demetri glanced to his right. His manager, Lloyd Kesler, may have needed a haircut, and an extreme fashion makeover, but when it came to negotiating deals, he was the best in the business. "No, I've been around. Just maxin' and relaxin'."

"Around, huh? Doing what?"

"You know, this and that." Demetri continued eating the barbecue chicken wings. They were onto him. He was sure of it. He couldn't do anything without this terrible threesome finding out, but he wasn't going to let anyone make him feel guilty for confronting Angela Kelly. The television newscaster had it coming to her. Or at least that was what he told himself when guilt tormented his conscience.

"Why are you giving me the third degree for being a couple minutes late?" Demetri said, choosing to stare at the mounted flat-screen TV instead of at his chubby, high-strung business manager. "I said I was sorry, man, so let it go. It's no big deal."

Nichola and Todd exchanged a worried glance, one he'd seen a million times over the years they'd all been working together, but it was Lloyd who spoke.

"You disregarded my advice and went down to WJN-TV station, didn't you?"

Demetri shrugged. "So, what if I did?"

"I told you I would handle it."

"You were taking too long," he said, shrugging his shoulders once more.

Nichola pointed a finger at him. "You went down to the TV station dressed like that?"

"What's wrong with my clothes?"

"Nothing if you're a street sweeper!" she quipped, laughing. "Why didn't you wear a suit? You look gorgeous in Armani, and you have the entire fall collection in your closet. I should know. I hung everything up when it arrived last week."

Demetri opened his mouth but quickly closed it. His team wouldn't understand. Every time he left the house, he felt as if there were a giant bull's-eye on his back, but with sunglasses, a baseball cap and workout gear on, no one recognized him. He could go about his business without pushy fans or sports reporters breathing down his neck. "To be honest, I didn't think much about what I put on," he lied.

"Well, you certainly fooled me." Todd snickered as he draped an arm along the back of the oversize booth. "I didn't recognize you when you walked in, and I've been your agent for more than a decade!"

"I didn't even know you owned sweatpants." Nichola's short strawberry-blond curls bounced all over her head as she laughed. "I thought you were a delivery guy!"

Good—my disguise worked, Demetri thought.

"I'm scared to even ask what happened down at the studio."

Lloyd looked stiff, like a statue in a wax museum. His eyes were narrowed so thin, Demetri couldn't see his pupils.

"What did Ms. Kelly say when you confronted her?"

A picture of the titillating newscaster flashed in Demetri's mind, and despite himself, a grin tickled his lips. "What *didn't* she say? The woman reamed me out, and at one point things got so heated, I thought she was going to give me a Chi-Town beat down!"

Todd chuckled and then said, "I really wish you hadn't gone over there, Demetri. You're supposed to be focusing on rehab and restoring the strength in your shoulder, not…"

Demetri's eyes wandered in the direction of the open kitchen. He spotted the waitress sashaying toward him, bread basket in hand, and licked his lips in hungry anticipation. When their eyes met, she stumbled and her legs buckled out from underneath her, sending the bread basket into the air. Dozens of buttered rolls shot across the shiny tiled floor.

Everyone at the table laughed, except Demetri.

"Are you okay?" Demetri slid out of the booth, clasped the waitress's forearm and slowly helped her to her feet. "You didn't hurt yourself, did you?"

"No, no, I'm okay…just *really* embarrassed."

"Here," he said, bending down. "Let me help you clean up."

Demetri gathered the discarded rolls, tossed them into the wicker basket and handed it back to her. "Be careful. These floors are slick," he warned, offering a reassuring smile. "I almost fell flat on my face the last time I was here!"

"I—I—I am *so* sorry, Mr. Morretti. It's my first day on the job, and I wasn't expecting to see you seated there."

"Baseball players have to eat, too, you know."

The redhead giggled. "Sorry again. I'll be right back with your order, Mr. Morretti."

"Call me Demetri. And good luck with the new job."

Smiling from ear to ear, she dashed back through the dining area and into the open kitchen.

"Don't forget the rolls!" Todd hollered, cupping his hands around his mouth. "And hurry up, tootsie! We don't have all day."

"Relax, man. She's new."

"Finish telling us about what happened at the station," Lloyd demanded, leaning forward in his seat. "I hope you kept your cool, because the last thing you need is any more bad press."

"Oh, I was as cool as an alley cat. Can't say the same for Ms. Kelly, though."

Nichola glanced up from her salad bowl. "You let her ream you out?"

"I let her rant and rave for a few minutes, and then I said my piece."

Todd gulped. "It sounds like your conversation was anything *but* peaceful."

"You can say that again," Lloyd mumbled, shaking his head.

Demetri finished chewing the food in his mouth and then continued. "I told Ms. Kelly if she didn't go on the air and apologize, I was going to sue her."

"You know that would be a waste of time and money, right? Not to mention—"

"Todd, I don't care," Demetri snapped, using a napkin to clean the sauce off his sticky fingers. "I'm sick of the media taking cheap shots at me and my family. If I don't take a stand now, the abuse will never end."

Nichola agreed. "I'm with you, Demetri. I think you should sue Angela Kelly. She's a bully, and you're not the only celebrity she's bad-mouthed on her show."

Demetri shot his publicist a grateful smile. He could always count on Nichola to go to bat for him. She went above and beyond her job description, made sure his day-to-day life ran smoothly. She kept the gold diggers—in his family and on the streets—at bay during the regular season so he could concentrate on his game. Nichola was more than just his publicist; she was a real, true friend.

"Once we finish up here, I'll give the station a call and see what they're willing to do."

"Don't bother, Lloyd. I met with the producer of Ms. Kelly's show, and she invited me to come on and do a live one-hour interview—"

"That's great!" Lloyd cheered, pumping his fist in the air. "You can set the record straight about all those crazy rumors floating around on the internet and plug your sponsors."

"And your charity work," Todd added. "That will get you the sympathy vote."

"I'm not doing the interview."

"What?" Lloyd made his eyes wide. "Why not?"

Nichola jumped in. "Because Angela Kelly's a vulture! She looks all nice and sweet, but she's cutthroat. Last week, she interviewed the pregnant girl on *NFL Wives,* and by the time the interview was done, the chick was in tears!"

"Yeah, probably because she felt guilty for screwing her sister's husband." Lloyd made a disgusted face. "I represent her ex, so I know the scoop. Trust me, she's no wallflower, and those tears weren't real. That woman was just playing it up for the cameras."

"Back to the matter at hand," Todd said, stealing a glance at his gold Rolex watch. "Demetri, please reconsider doing the interview. Angela Kelly isn't going to double-cross you. And just to make sure she doesn't try to pull a fast one on us, I'll be on set watch—"

Demetri cut his agent off midword. "Still not interested. Drop it."

Todd held his hands up high in the air like an unarmed man surrendering to the police. "All right, all right, you're the boss. I won't mention it again."

"Good." Demetri leaned back in the booth and calmly

addressed Nichola. "I want you to call Salem Velasquez at WJN-TV and politely decline her offer."

Nichola gave a thumbs-up sign. "I'll call her when I get back to the office."

The food arrived, and their discussion came to an abrupt halt.

Picking up his utensils, Demetri bowed his head and said a quick word of grace. He was starving, but he ate his food slowly, savoring each tasty bite. The conversation turned to his weekly agenda, his newest sponsorship deals and the upcoming Caribbean cruise he was planning for eighty-five of his family members and friends. He traveled with his family every year, and every year, the trip caused Demetri enormous stress. Thankfully, Nichola was overseeing all of the pertinent details of the three-week vacation in August and keeping his most unruly relatives in line.

"There are a few things I need to run by you." Nichola set aside her salad bowl and retrieved her iPad from her designer purse. "As you know, the Demetri Morretti Foundation is having a Fourth of July extravaganza this summer, but so far I've only heard back from a handful of celebrities. You're going to have to call some of your superstar friends and extend a personal invitation."

"Nichola, why can't you do it?"

"Because I'm not the slugger with the golden arm. You are!"

Everyone chuckled.

"We're doing it real big this year," Nichola declared. "We're having magicians, flamethrowers, a dunk tank and even circus performers. To keep everything on track, I booked celebrity event planner Claudia Jeffries-Medina. And award-winning photographer Kenyon Blake will be on hand to capture every heartfelt moment."

"It sounds like the Demetri Morretti Foundation is throwing one hell of a party!" Todd said with a grin.

"The more press we get to cover the event the better." Nichola rested a hand on Demetri's forearm. "I'm going to need you to be nice to the media from here on out. No more arguments with Angela Kelly or anyone else who rubs you the wrong way."

I'd let that sexy newscaster rub me the right *way all night long.* Demetri shook his head in an attempt to remove the insane thought from his mind. Angela Kelly was the enemy, a woman who took great pride in humiliating him, and he wasn't even remotely interested in her.

Then why are you thinking about all the wicked things you'd like to do to her in bed? his inner voice jeered.

"Demetri, if you want this event to be a success, you'll have to be that fun, personable guy we all know and love."

"It's hard to be in a jovial mood when perfect strangers are snapping pictures of me in the bathroom and the paparazzi is trailing me around town."

Nichola wore a sympathetic smile. "Just remember this event is for a good cause. Last year, we raised over a half a million dollars for the foundation, and this year I'm hoping to triple that number."

Her words made Demetri grin, filling him with pride. That was what it was all about. Making a difference in someone's life. Being famous definitely had its good points, and now, thanks to his new multimillion-dollar contract, he could help even more children in need. "Thanks for overseeing everything," he said, feeling bad for snapping at her earlier. "As usual, it sounds like you have everything under control."

"Now," Todd said, "all we need are some celebrity faces to give the event star power!"

"Speaking of star power, I received dozens of letters from local area schools this week." Nichola took a stack of envelopes out of her purse and showed them to Demetri. "Are you interested in speaking at any of these functions?"

Demetri thought for a moment. As far as he knew, he had

nothing planned for the month. But if he went to the career-day events, there was a good chance someone would tip off the media, and he'd arrive to find a mob of fans and paparazzi. This was a main reason Demetri avoided public events. Because of his wealth, and the poor choices he'd made in the past, he was an easy target, and these days he couldn't go anywhere without some young punk looking to start a fight. "Tell the organizers I can't make it, but send each school a check."

"For the same amount as last year?"

"Double it."

Lloyd's jaw hit his flabby chest with a thud. "B-but, Demetri, that's over two hundred thousand dollars to each school. A million dollars total."

"I know, Lloyd. I did the math."

"I'll ensure your accountant sends out the checks today," Nichola said, typing furiously on her iPad. "And I'll make sure to tip my source at the *Tribune* about your *very* generous donation to five inner-city schools."

"No, don't. It's nobody's business how much I give." Demetri's expression turned serious. He'd learned early on in his career it was better to leave some things private. He didn't want anyone—especially his relatives—to hear how much he gave to charity. He could almost hear the outlandish things they would request if they knew. "Keep it quiet, Nichola. The less people who know the better."

"But it would be great press," she argued. "And a touchy, feel-good story even someone like Angela Kelly would love!"

At the mention of the newscaster's name, he remembered their heated argument that morning at the studio. He told himself to stop thinking about Angela Kelly, to forget they'd ever met, but he couldn't get her pretty brown eyes and her toned, curvy shape out of his mind.

After leaving the television station, he'd returned to his car and turned on his cell phone. Instead of reading his newest text messages, he'd opened the internet and searched her name, clicking on the first link that popped up. He read Angela Kelly's bio, then watched an hour's worth of her most popular interviews. Most of them were with celebrities—actors, singers, professional athletes and supermodels. But Angela was so engaging, and witty, she looked like a star in her own right. There were dozens of pictures of her, at various events in and around town, and in each photograph she looked like a million bucks *and* had a different date.

What's up with that? Demetri quickly told himself he didn't care. And he didn't. His mother had always warned him against falling for pretty money-hungry types. And from the day he was drafted in the major leagues, gold diggers had been throwing themselves at him left, right and center. Feisty, headstrong women—like Angela Kelly—where by far the worst type.

Tasting his wine, he hoped the savory drink eased his troubled mind. Demetri closed his eyes and saw Angela Kelly glaring at him. He gave his head a hard shake. He had to quit wondering how many guys she was dating and if she had a lover, because after today he had no intention of ever seeing her again—unless it was in civil court.

Chapter 4

Angela stormed inside her best friend's kitchen, dumped her purse on the granite countertop and paced the length of the room, gesturing wildly with her hands. "I'm so angry I could scream!"

"Well, please don't," Simone Young said, glancing into the living room. "The boys just fell asleep, and if you wake them, I'll kill you."

Angela blew out a deep breath and counted to ten. On the drive over from the WJN-TV station, she'd relived every second of her argument with Demetri and the subsequent meeting with her boss. It didn't matter which way Angela looked at it—she felt cheated. As if Salem had thrown her under the bus.

"Now, what's got you all riled up?" Simone closed the dishwasher and then leaned against it. Rubbing a hand over her baby bump, she cocked her head to the side and frowned. "Did that sleazy sportscaster proposition you again?"

"No. Worse."

"I can't imagine anything worse than being propositioned by a guy who drives a lemon *and* still lives at home with his mama!"

A giggle tickled the back of Angela's throat. Leave it to Simone to make her laugh in the midst of a crisis. That was why she'd driven across town in rush hour to see her. They'd been friends ever since meeting on the University of Chicago campus ten years ago, and Angela loved Simone like a sister. The busy wife and mother could make her forget her problems, even if just for a few minutes. And now more than ever, Angela needed her advice. "Hakeem's not that bad. Just annoying. I can handle him."

"I'm all for keeping the peace at work, but I would have spoken to HR about his unwanted advances months ago."

"And have everyone at the station turn against me? No, thanks. The lead anchor hates me, so the few friends I have, I'd like to keep."

"Do you want a cup of ginger tea?"

"Yeah, but put some vodka in mine."

Simone opened the cupboard, took out two ceramic mugs and waddled over to the kettle. "I swear, Angela, sometimes you're just too much."

"What? I need some alcohol to steady my nerves. I've had the day from hell!"

"Girl, please. You work at a TV station and tape your show in a warm, cozy studio." Simone handed Angela a mug, then sat down at the table in front of her laptop and social-work case files. "Come down to my agency, and I'll show you what a bad day *really* looks like." Sliding her hands around her mug, Simone raised it to her mouth and took a sip. "I'm trying not to let anything stress me out," she confessed, gazing down at her belly, "but it's hard being pregnant, taking care of my family *and* doing my job effectively."

"God, I am such a bad friend! I came barging in here and didn't even ask how your doctor's appointment went this morning." Angela took the seat across from Simone and squeezed her hand. "How are the babies doing?"

Her grin lit up the kitchen. "They're good. Gaining weight and kicking me like crazy!"

Angela listened to Simone recount every detail of her ultrasound appointment and, for a split second, wondered what it would be like to be pregnant. Back when she was a naive nineteen-year-old, madly in love with her college sweetheart, she'd had dreams of getting married and raising a family. But after countless arguments about her career, he'd dumped her via email and moved on to greener pastures. *Younger, thinner pastures,* Angela thought, recalling the day she'd bumped into her ex and his new girlfriend at the mall. Her ex had foolishly thought he could control every aspect of her life, and although it stung to see him with someone else, Angela knew she was better off without him.

The whole male species, actually.

Since moving back to Chicago six months ago, Angela had been playing the field and loving every minute of it. She never went out with the same guy twice, and although she'd earned a reputation of being a heartbreaker, she had no intention of ever settling down. She'd leave getting married, having babies and watching cartoons to her love-struck girlfriends.

"So what's going on with you?" Simone asked. "What's got you all worked up?"

"Demetri Morretti showed up at the station today and demanded that I go on the air and apologize to him," Angela said, the words tumbling out of her mouth in one long gush. "Can you believe it? I mean, really, who does he think he is?"

"Well, you did call him a spoiled, immature athlete on national television…"

"None of this would have happened if the security guards had been doing their job," she continued. "They should be fired."

"It was bound to happen, Angela. You couldn't avoid Demetri Morretti forever."

"I knew some of the players were upset, but I never expected Demetri to show up at the station. I almost fell over when I saw him, and when he started in on me, I lost it." Angela shook her head at the memory of their heated confrontation. "It was horrible, Simone. We were yelling and arguing and dissing each other."

"I know. I saw *and* I heard."

"You saw and you heard what?"

"Your showdown with Demetri. The video was posted online about an hour ago."

"Online?" she repeated, shaking her head. "As in on the internet?"

"Yup. Sexy Chicago Newscaster Goes Off on Baseball Superstar, and since it's gone viral, it's received thousands of hits." Simone slid the laptop in front of Angela, clicked on the appropriate link and said, "See for yourself."

Angela gasped when she saw her image on the screen. "H-h-how come Demetri looks all calm, cool and collected and I look like a raving lunatic?" she stammered, unable to believe her eyes. In the heat of the moment, Angela felt as if Demetri was attacking her, but that hadn't been the case at all. He was chill, at ease, and his tone was so soft, she could barely hear what he was saying. Unfortunately, she heard her curt, clipped tone loud and clear.

"I'm going to be the laughingstock of late-night television!" she wailed.

Simone put her hands on Angela's shoulder. "Girl, it's not that bad."

"You're right. It's worse."

"Look on the bright side—"

"There isn't one."

"Yes, there is." Simone tapped the computer screen. "You're working the hell out of your new Chanel shorts suit, and all those sessions with your personal trainer are definitely paying off because your booty looks good!"

"You're not helping, Simone."

"And as usual, you're being overly dramatic."

"No, I'm not." Angela cringed when she heard the note of despair in her voice, but she couldn't help the way she was feeling. Being secretly recorded unnerved her, but having the video posted online, for the whole world to see, made Angela want to curl into a ball in the middle of the kitchen floor. "I want to be taken seriously as a journalist, and this whole episode with Demetri is only going to set me back."

"Or it could catapult you to stardom, and you could end up with your own reality show!"

Angela gave her best friend a blank stare.

"What? Throwing a tantrum on camera has worked for dozens of other stars. I don't see why it can't work for you."

"Why would someone waste their time uploading this stupid video on YouTube?"

"Probably just for kicks. People post all sorts of wacky things online these days."

Angela winced and then dropped her face in her hands.

"Sorry, girl. That's not what I meant."

"But that's exactly how I look. Wacky," she admitted, swallowing a sob. "I bet Demetri posted the video to get back at me, to make me look like a fool."

"You think so?"

Angela gave it more thought and considered exactly what had transpired between them that afternoon. "I don't know. He had no way of knowing what would happen, but I wouldn't put it past him. He's surly and bitter, and this sort of thing is right up his alley."

"So, what happened after your boss ordered you into her office?"

Angela told Simone an abbreviated version of her terse ten-minute meeting with Salem. She admitted being so wound up after her argument with Demetri, she couldn't concentrate on what her boss was saying. But she did vividly remember Salem inviting the baseballer on her show. "I can't believe Salem invited him to appear on my show!"

"I don't understand why you're mad. Having Demetri Morretti on your show will send your ratings through the roof!" Simone said, throwing her hands up in the air. "For some reason, people love to hate that guy, and since he hasn't done a sit-down interview in years, viewers will tune in. I don't even like baseball, but I'd definitely watch!"

"I'd rather have a mime on my show than Demetri Morretti."

"No one said you had to play nice, Angela. Do the interview *your* way," she advised. "Put him in the hot seat. Ask tough questions. That's what viewers want to see. Good, hard interviews with today's hottest stars."

Nodding her head slowly, she considered her best friend's advice. Angela knew if she grilled Demetri Morretti on air, her boss and everyone in the production team would be licking their chops. "Simone, you're brilliant!"

"I know. That's what I keep telling my husband, but he doesn't believe me!"

The women laughed.

"I better get started on dinner." Standing, Simone gathered her case files and dumped them into her briefcase. "Marcus will be home soon, and I still haven't seasoned the chicken."

Angela watched her girlfriend, moving anxiously around the kitchen, and was glad she didn't have to rush home to cook dinner for a man. *If I ever get married, my husband will cook for* me, she decided.

"You didn't touch your tea," Simone said. "Do you want me to reheat it?"

"Sure, and don't forget the vodka this time!"

Simone raised her eyebrows.

"What? I'm stressed-out," Angela argued, feeling the need to defend herself. "I want *Eye on Chicago* to do well so I can move on to bigger and better things, but I hate the thought of having Demetri Morretti on my show. The guy's creepy."

"Yeah, creepy *fine*," Simone quipped, ambling over to the microwave. She put the mug inside and hit Start. "I read in *Forbes* magazine that his new mansion is so big, he needs a helicopter to get him from one end to the other!"

Angela's eyes strayed back to the computer. For some

reason, she couldn't stop thinking about Demetri. He had a dreamy look and such a compelling presence, he could give a perfectly healthy woman asthma. Long after he'd stalked out of her studio, Angela was still thinking about how good he smelled, how broad his shoulders were and how sexy he looked in his workout gear.

"The guy is so frickin' hot, actresses and pop stars are constantly fighting over him!"

Scowling, Angela took the mug Simone offered her and cradled it in her hands. "I don't see why. He's a pain in the ass. And rude, too."

"Girl, don't hate. Demetri Morretti is the hottest thing in sports right now and for good reason. He's guest starred on a slew of TV shows, hosted *Saturday Night Live,* and he's been on the cover of dozens of magazines, as well."

Angela raised an eyebrow and studied her best friend closely. "For someone who doesn't like baseball, you sure know a lot about the guy."

"It's not my fault. My husband's a sports addict, and he thinks Demetri's mad cool," Simone explained, opening the fridge and grabbing a bag of mixed vegetables. "They've worked out together a few times at Samson's and really hit it off."

"Why didn't you say anything?"

"Girl, please, with all I've got going on I can barely remember what day of the week it is, let alone who Marcus trains on a daily basis."

"The fifteenth can't come fast enough," Angela said, slumping down into her chair. "I'm really looking forward to us hanging out and cutting loose. It's long overdue."

Simone glanced up from the marble cutting board. "We have plans for Friday?"

"Ah, yeah. We're going to the grand opening of Dolce Vita, remember?" Angela shot her friend a funny look. "I'm covering the event for the station, but I should be done and ready to party by eight—nine at the latest."

"Sorry, girl, but I can't go. Marcus has the weekend off, and he's taking me away for a few days," she explained, a girlie smile exploding onto her face.

"What are you going to do with the boys?" Angela asked. "Cart them off to your mother-in-law's house again?"

"You know it!"

The friends laughed.

"I never dreamed Gladys and I would be close, but ever since I got pregnant, she's gone out of her way to help me," Simone confessed. "She never follows the boys' schedule, but she'll babysit at a moment's notice and always encourages me to take time out for myself."

Angela concealed a grin. "I'm glad you and Gladys worked out your differences, because you're *really* going to need her help when you get pregnant with baby number five and six!"

"No way. After I have these girls, I'm done. It's your turn to be barefoot and pregnant."

"I'm not having children, remember?"

"Why not?" Wrinkling her nose, her lips pursed, she placed a hand on her hip. "You're great with my boys and the kids at the shelter love you. Even the teenagers. And everyone knows, teenagers hate everybody!"

"That's different. The kids at the shelter don't have anybody else."

"Good with kids is good with kids. It doesn't matter if they're yours or not," Simone argued. "You can have a career *and* a family, Angela. It doesn't have to be one or the other."

"It does for me."

"That's because you're a perfectionist with implausibly high standards."

"And proud of it," Angela said. *I'm going to make it to the top and no one is going to stop me,* she decided, as an idea began taking shape in her mind. Tomorrow, she'd tell Salem she was on board to do the interview and submit a list of fake questions. Questions she had no intention of asking Demetri Morretti on the air.

A smirk tickled her lips. By the time Angela was finished with the baseball star, he'd be toast, and she'd be the talk of the town. And one step closer to sliding into that lead-anchor chair. Angela was going to take the news world by storm, and she wasn't letting anyone—especially a sly superstar athlete with a chiseled physique—get in her way.

Chapter 5

"You need to change your name to Trouble," a voice boomed, drowning out the hip-hop song playing inside Samson's Gym, "because everywhere you go, trouble seems to find you!"

Demetri cast a glance over his shoulder at his former teammate and workout buddy T. J. Nicks. Unable to hold the weight any longer, Demetri dropped the barbell on the floor and plopped down on the workout bench.

Samson's Gym, a state-of-the-art fitness center frequented by pro athletes, college students and moneyed professionals, was usually packed, but this morning there was only a handful of people working out. An older man, who looked as if he was on the verge of collapse, was lifting weights a few benches over, but he was so focused on his routine, he was oblivious to the world. And that was how Demetri liked it. As long as he kept his head down and didn't make eye contact with anyone, no one would recognize him and he could work out in peace.

"I haven't seen you in a minute," Demetri said, swiping his towel off the side of the workout bench and wiping the sweat off his face. "What's up?"

"You tell me."

Shrugging a shoulder, he readjusted his baseball cap. "Nothing much."

"Are you sure? From what I hear, you've been a very busy boy."

"You saw the video?"

A grin fell across T.J.'s dark, narrow face. "Sure did. One of my boys emailed it to me. I almost died laughing when that gorgeous newscaster from WJN-TV called you a spoiled, overgrown kid who needed a time-out!"

Demetri chuckled, though at the time, when Angela was giving him a verbal smackdown, he didn't feel like laughing. He hadn't felt like lashing back at her, either. Maybe because his eyes were glued to her lips, and her scent was a bold, exotic fragrance that aroused his senses. One week after his infamous showdown with Angela Kelly, and he was still thinking about her. Demetri loved his mom, but he blamed her for his present state of mind. If she hadn't called him last night from Italy and reamed him out for disrespecting Angela at her studio, he wouldn't be thinking about the sexy TV newscaster now. He didn't know why Angela had someone record their conversation, and post it online, but he intended to ask her. Demetri didn't care what his mother said. He wasn't a bully. Angela Kelly was a liar who had it coming to her.

"Are you here to work out or gossip?" Demetri asked.

"Both. You know ribbing you is the highlight of my day!" Chuckling, T.J. bent down and retied the laces of his white sneakers. "Why aren't you working out at your home gym? Having it renovated again?"

"No, I needed a change of scenery."

"Shoot, if I had a home gym like yours, I'd never leave the house!"

Demetri picked up his titanium sports bottle, unscrewed the lid and took a long drink of water. T.J. was a good friend, and he'd never put Demetri's business out on the street, but he wasn't going to tell him the truth. The real reason he was there, at seven o'clock in the morning, was to talk to Angela Kelly. Thanks to the owner of the gym, Demetri knew what days and times Angela worked out with her personal trainer. To ensure he didn't oversleep, he'd set every alarm clock in his house and asked his personal assistant to phone him just in case. Now he was at the gym, waiting for her to make an appearance. He only hoped this time when they spoke, she wouldn't go off on him.

"How is rehab going?" T.J. asked, striding over to the free weights and selecting a set of dumbbells. "Think you might make it back in time for the play-offs?"

"I hope so, but I doubt it. It kills me not being out there with my team, but my surgeon wants me to take the rest of the season off, and I'm not going to disregard his advice. The last time I did, I ended up tearing a ligament in my knee, and that hurt like a bitch."

"I hear you, man. What's next on your circuit?"

Yawning, Demetri stood and stretched his hands lazily above his head. "I'm going to do a couple laps around the track, then cool down in the sauna."

"Really? You look like you're about to fall asleep." T.J. wore a quizzical look. "Why are you here so early, anyways? You never get out of bed before noon."

Demetri thought fast and said the first thing that popped into his mind. "I'll be tied up the rest of the day, so I decided to get my training out of the way now."

Eyes wide, T.J. dropped the dumbbells back on the rack and gestured to the cardio room. "Dude, guess who just strode up in here looking like my next baby mama. Angela-sexy-as-sin-Kelly!" he hollered, eagerly rubbing his hands together. "I've met a lot of gorgeous girls, but that honey takes the cake. She's hot, successful and crazy-smart."

"Sounds like somebody has a crush," Demetri teased, poking fun.

"Who doesn't? She's one of the baddest chicks around!"

Demetri wore a blank face. He didn't want his friend or anyone else to know that he was feeling Angela Kelly. He had a knack for picking the wrong woman, and the TV newscaster was everything he *didn't* want in a girlfriend. From now on, he was staying away from fame-loving, celebrity-obsessed types. His ex, a wildly popular R & B singer with a good-girl image, had gone to extraordinary lengths to keep their relationship a secret. But Demetri was through with secret phone calls, ducking out back doors and clandestine meetings in hotel rooms across town. He'd just have to fight his attraction to Angela Kelly, because hooking up with the feisty, headstrong sister was asking for trouble. "She's all right," he said with a shrug. "Too prissy for me, though."

"All right?" When T.J.'s jaw dropped, his tongue fell out of his open mouth. "Man, please. Angela Kelly is a dime piece and you know it!"

Spotting Angela inside the cardio room, Demetri admired her shapely physique. He liked to see tall, athletic women in bright, figure-hugging workout clothes. He loved how the TV newscaster's yellow shirt and fitted leggings showed off her curves.

Demetri told himself to look away, but his eyes were glued to Angela's big, beautiful backside. And when she bent over and touched her toes, all the blood drained from his head. Swallowing hard, he gulped down the rest of his water.

"Quit frontin', man." T.J. leveled a finger at him. "You're hot for Angela, too, just like every other guy in Chi-Town. You're just scared of getting shot down."

Demetri shook his head. "She's not my type."

"Yeah, right!"

"If I wanted Angela Kelly, I could have her, but I don't, so—"

"No offense, bro, but she's *way* out of your league."

Now Demetri was the one with wide eyes. "I'm not trying to brag, T.J., but I'm one of the highest-paid athletes in baseball," he said, feeling the need to defend himself. "Money is no object, man. You know that."

"Yeah, but you know how you are with your money."

"No, I don't. How am I?"

"Cheap, cheap, cheap," he chirped, shielding his mouth

with the back of his hand. "You signed a blockbuster deal a
few months back, but you live like a struggling college student!"

"I'm not cheap. I just don't believe in wasting money."
Demetri stepped out onto the track. "I have no intention of
blowing through my earnings and being broke in ten years."

"Is that why you force your personal shopper to clip cou-
pons and comparison shop?"

"No," he argued with a laugh. "My mom ordered her to!"

Chuckling, the men jogged the length of track at a smooth,
fluid pace.

"Word on the street is that Angela only dates rich guys,"
T.J. explained, his tone matter-of-fact. "You know, men who
can wine her, dine her and pay her expenses."

Demetri frowned. He found it hard to believe that Angela
Kelly was a kept woman. She didn't strike him as the kind
of girl who'd expect a man to support her, but what did he
know about women? If he knew more about the species, he
wouldn't keep getting played. All of his ex-girlfriends were
more interested in his celebrity status than having a real,
meaningful relationship with him. And at thirty-two, that
was exactly what Demetri was looking for. He knew he was
a great catch and he wanted to catch a great woman. Someone
who would be there when his career ended and the endorse-
ment deals dried up. His teammates told him he was lucky to
be single, but Demetri didn't agree. He envied the guys who
got off the team bus and had their wives and children waiting for them. One-night stands left him feeling empty inside,
and contrary to what his older brothers, Nicco and Rafael,
told him, a warm, curvy body didn't make everything better.

"You dumped the last girl who demanded you buy her a
mansion in Bel Air, and that Hawaiian chick for stealing your
underwear and selling them on eBay, so there's no way you
and Angela Kelly would ever work out."

"Good, because I'm not interested in her," he tossed back.

"But if you were, you could do her, right?"

Demetri wet his lips with his tongue. The thought of sexing Angela, on his custom-made bed, with soft jazz music playing in the background and scented candles flickering around the room, made a slow, lazy smile break out across his mouth. "No comment."

T.J. raised his eyebrows. "Oh, so you think she'd be putty in your hands?"

An explicit image of Angela—naked and rocking her shapely hips against his erection—flashed in Demetri's mind, derailing his thoughts. He couldn't shake the picture from his mind, and when they jogged past the cardio room, and Demetri saw Angela performing squat thrusts, his erection came to life. "I never said that, T.J."

"It was implied."

"Angela Kelly is just like every other girl. Willing to do whatever it takes to bed a baller so she can enjoy his status *and* his checkbook."

"Care to make a friendly wager?" T.J. stuck his hands into his track pants, took out a few hundred-dollar bills and waved them under Demetri's nose. "A thousand bucks says you don't get past first base with that sexy TV newscaster."

"Knock it off, man. We're not in grade school, and betting about women is juvenile."

"Scared you're going to lose, huh? You should be. Angela Kelly is a hard nut to crack."

Demetri believed him. The newscaster was a fiery, passionate woman with a sharp tongue, and there was nothing soft or genteel about her. His eyes trailed her around the cardio room, and when she hopped off the treadmill and toweled off, Demetri knew it was time to make his move. "Be right back," he said, spinning around and jogging backward. "See you in five."

"Where are you going?"

Demetri wore a crooked smile. "To settle a score."

* * *

"I—I—I think I'm dying." Gasping for air, Angela fanned a hand in front of her face and slumped against the wall like a sack of potatoes. "Everything hurts, even my butt, and I didn't sit down once during our session!"

"That's because plyometric workouts engage all of the major muscle groups in the body." Her personal trainer, a stocky man with thick dreadlocks, patted her on the shoulder. "You did awesome today, Angela. Way to go pushing yourself through that last rep of weights."

"Great—tell that to the E.R. doctor when he wheels me into the operating room."

"I'll see you on Thursday."

"If I don't die between now and then." Too tired to wave, she closed her eyes and breathed deeply through her nose. It was the first time all week she hadn't thought about her run-in with Demetri Morretti or her problems with her brother, Rodney. But now that her treacherous hour-long training session was over, all her troubling thoughts came rushing back. Demetri had posted a scathing message about her on his blog, and all morning she'd been fielding calls from the media. Angela wanted to report the news, not *be* the news, and it annoyed her that she'd become a hot topic.

Her legs felt like rubber, but she staggered over to the water fountain, one aching step at a time. Placing her bottle underneath the spout, she pressed the lever and leaned against the wall. Angela stared out onto the track. Her gaze wandered aimlessly around the gym before landing on a fit, muscled specimen in a sleeveless Chicago Royals T-shirt and knee-length shorts.

For the second time in minutes, Angela let out a deep-seated groan. Her eyes ate up every inch of the stranger's towering frame. The square jaw, the rack of his shoulders, his bulging biceps. Since high school, she'd had a weakness for strong, athletic guys, and Mr. Man was definitely her type. All lean and rugged, he looked like the kind of guy who could fix the leaky faucet in her kitchen *and* rock her world in the bedroom.

Angela felt ice-cold water flow down her hands and snapped out of her thoughts. Releasing the lever, she tucked her water bottle under her arm and dabbed her wristband over her damp cheeks. She glanced over her shoulder, to ensure no one had witnessed her reaction, and there, standing a few feet away, was Demetri Morretti. *Damn.* He was the same guy she'd been drooling over on the track seconds earlier.

Angela sucked in a breath. Her pulse soared, and her heartbeat drummed so loud in her ears, she couldn't think. Physically active and fit her entire life, she'd never had any problems with her heart, but every time Demetri Morretti was around, it throbbed, skipped and beat out of control. Like right now.

"Good morning," he said, tipping his baseball cap at her. "Can we talk?"

His voice was husky and matched his gruff disposition. He looked angry, and pained, as if someone had just beaten him in an arm wrestle.

"I think you said enough the other day at the TV station, don't you?"

"I'm sorry I barged into your studio."

"You should be."

"You're right, and I shouldn't have stepped to you like that, either. It won't happen again."

His gaze probed her eyes, one terrifying second at a time. Admitting he'd made a mistake couldn't have been easy, and Angela found herself moved by the sincerity of his tone. But not enough to forgive him for what he'd written about her on his blog yesterday.

"I was hoping we could start over."

"Let's not and say we did," Angela quipped.

"I knew you were going to make this hard for me."

She puzzled over Demetri's words but decided not to question him. Angela had zero interest in patching things up with the conceited baseball star but knew better than to argue with him in public again. There was no telling who was watching. Or secretly taping them. And the last thing Angela wanted was another video of her screaming at Demetri Morretti to mysteriously surface online. "I don't have anything to say to you."

"If anyone should be holding a grudge, it should be me," he said, pointing an index finger at his chest. "Because of you, I'm the most hated athlete in America."

"Don't kid yourself, Morretti. Your reputation was in the dumps long before my *Athletes Behaving Badly* story."

"Well, your report certainly didn't help."

"Neither did your six-game batting slump."

His face, like his voice, was stern and tense. "I didn't come over here to argue. I came here to apologize for what happened the other day."

"You have some nerve. First, you post a nasty message about me on your blog—"

"My blog?" Demetri looked puzzled, as confused as a driver who'd exited a store and forgotten where he'd parked, but when he spoke, his words were measured and his speech was slow. "I don't blog or Tweet or post online messages. My publicist manages all of my social-media accounts."

"But the blog is in your name."

"I know," he said with a shrug of his broad shoulders, "but I'm not much of a computer person. I prefer talking to people face-to-face, *especially* beautiful TV newscasters."

Angela felt a smile claim her lips but washed it off. She wasn't ready to forgive and forget what Demetri had done, but she believed he didn't write his blog. It didn't sound like something a guy would write. Most celebrities didn't post online messages or respond directly to fans, but the smart ones were wise enough to preapprove what their handlers put on the web. But obviously Demetri Morretti was too busy getting into bar fights to care. "A guy could get in a lot of trouble letting other people speak for him."

"No one speaks for me. I speak for myself."

"Could have fooled me." Her confidence kicked in and stamped out the unruly butterflies flittering around her stomach. "You're just full of surprises this morning, aren't you? Next, you'll be telling me you didn't have someone record our argument and post it online."

"I didn't. Actually, I thought *you* did."

"Are you kidding me?" Angela gave a bitter laugh. "Why would I post a video that made me look crazier than the Joker?"

His scowl fell away when he chuckled. It was the first time Angela had ever seen or heard Demetri laugh, and she liked the sound. Immensely. Angela caught herself and quit giggling. He was the enemy, a man bent on destroying her, not someone she could trust. She'd never been a play-it-safe kind of girl, but whenever Demetri was around, her guard went up.

"Let's call a truce," he suggested, offering his right hand. "You stop bashing me on your show, and I'll promise not to come back to your studio. Deal?"

Angela paused. She was ready to bury the hatchet, but when she remembered his Facebook post—the one that said *Talentless newscasters who sleep their way to the top shouldn't throw stones*—she came to her senses. Her gut instincts told her Demetri was behind the post. Had to be. He was the one who hated her, not his stupid flunkies. "Sorry," she said, wearing an innocent face. "I don't make deals with the devil."

Then Angela spun around and stalked into the ladies' changing room.

Chapter 6

Angela stepped inside her two-bedroom town house, immediately seeing the enormous framed photograph hanging in the foyer, and smiled to herself. It didn't matter how long her day was—one look at the picture of her and her friends sipping cocktails on a Fiji beach, and her frustrations melted away.

Dumping her keys on the front table, she dropped her work bag on the floor and kicked off her leather pumps. Entering her living room and seeing her chic home furnishings filled Angela with pride. *My swanky bachelorette pad deserves a spread in* Home Decor *magazine,* she thought, collapsing onto her cozy red velvet couch. Her house was inundated with bright colors, unique artifacts she'd scored from her travels abroad and cute, cozy furniture. Purchasing her first home, in a neighborhood she loved, was one of Angela's greatest accomplishments. On warm, sunny days she loved to sit on the porch and chat with her neighbors.

But not today.

Her run-in with Demetri Morretti yesterday morning at Samson's Gym consumed her thoughts and weighed so heavily on her. It was all she had been thinking about. Stretching her legs out in front of her, she allowed the sunshine streaming through the windows to quiet her mind. The tree-lined street was overrun with kids. They were riding bikes, splashing in puddles and doing cartwheels across their lawns. On any other day, their shrieks of laughter would draw her outside to cheer them on, but tonight Angela didn't have the energy to move.

Unzipping her tweed blazer, she shrugged it off and chucked it at the end of the couch. After work, she'd stopped by Simone's house for dinner, and after two hearty servings of vegetable lasagna, and a couple of strawberry wine coolers, she was stuffed.

Picking up the remote, she pointed it at the TV and hit the on button. Angela flipped channels, in the hopes of finding something funny to watch, something that would take her mind off of her troubles. Angela spotted the clip of her arguing with Demetri playing on a rival news station and pounded the sofa cushions with her fists. "I can't believe WQK is showing this stupid video again!" she raged, her chest heaving with anger. "Those jerks!"

Sitting in her living room, watching the video for the umpteenth time, Angela wondered how she could spin her showdown with Demetri into an even bigger news story. Not one that had people pointing fingers or laughing at her. Rather, a story that would drive more viewers to check out her weekly show.

As the clip played, Angela found herself admiring Demetri's long, lean frame. He looked as cool as a gun-slinging cowboy, and although he was glaring at her during the entire video, there was no disputing the baseballer's striking good looks. With his smooth skin and dark, striking eyes, Demetri Morretti could land a role in any big-budget Hollywood movie. And it would be a guaranteed smash hit at the box office.

Angela heard the telephone ringing on the table behind her but decided to let the answering machine pick it up. She wasn't in the mood to talk. It was probably one of her single girlfriends calling to ask about Demetri Morretti, and Angela was sick and tired of hearing the man's name. In the past week, the video had received thousands of hits, and according to Simone's husband, it was still making the rounds of the local radio stations and was a hot topic on *Sports Chicago*.

Angela released a deep sigh. By now, anyone who didn't live under a rock had heard about her showdown with Demetri Morretti. And even though Angela knew the story made sensational headlines and would drum up free publicity for her show, she was embarrassed over the way she'd acted. In the video, she was loud and brash and looked completely out of control. That wasn't her. In all her years of working in television, Angela had never gone off on a guest, never lost her cool. But there was something about Demetri Morretti that brought out the worst in her. And that scared her. What if he agreed to do her show and she lost her temper again? Would she even have a show when the dust cleared?

Angela heard her cell phone buzz, and she fished it out of her nearby purse. She scanned the screen for the number and released a deep sigh when she saw the Denver area code. It was her dad, calling from the road. He never called to chitchat, and was an avid sports fan, so she knew he was phoning to find out if she'd lost her damn mind. "Hey, Dad," she said, faking a cheerful voice. "How are you doing?"

"Angela, what happened with Demetri Morretti?"

So much for easing into the conversation, she thought, raking a hand through her hair.

"Dad, it was nothing."

"It sure looked like a whole lot of something to me."

Biting the inside of her lip, she racked her brain for a plausible explanation for why she'd gone off on baseball's biggest star.

"Quit stalling, baby girl, and tell me what happened."

At his words, Angela smiled. Her father, Cornelius Kelly, had raised her and her brother single-handedly. He had never once complained or bad-mouthed her absentee mother. And when her mother died from a drug overdose, it was her dad who helped her overcome her grief. A proud daddy's girl, Angela grew up doing all the things her father loved. To this day, Angela consulted her dad before making any major decisions and lived for the afternoons they spent jogging around Millennium Park, watching their beloved Chicago Royals play or barbecuing at her childhood home. Her dad was a truck driver who worked long hours for crummy pay, and as soon as Angela became lead anchor at WJN-TV, she was going to pay off his bills and buy him a new car.

"Demetri Morretti showed up unexpectedly at WJN-TV."

"And," Cornelius prompted.

"And when he confronted me over my *Athletes Behaving Badly* segment, I lost it," Angela confessed, forcing the bitter truth out of her mouth. "I know the athletes mentioned in the story are upset, but I never expected Demetri Morretti to pop up at the studio, demanding an apology. Seeing him threw me for a loop."

"Morretti didn't put his hands on you, did he?"

"God, no!" she hollered. "If he had, I would have slugged him!"

"That's my girl!"

"Dad, I'm…" Angela struggled with her words. Swallowing, she pushed past her emotions and spoke from her heart. "Dad, I'm sorry if what I did embarrassed you. I got caught up in the moment, and—"

"I'm not mad at you, baby girl. I'm damn proud!"

"You are?"

"Of course. It's about time someone stood up to Demetri Morretti, and I'm glad that my smart, beautiful daughter was the one to do it."

Angela sat up straight. "You really mean that?"

"I sure do!" His strong voice boomed through the phone. "It's not your fault you lost your temper. Demetri Morretti provoked you, didn't he?"

Angela stayed silent. She wasn't going to defend Demetri Morretti—he was the enemy—so instead of correcting her dad, she vented her frustration. "Dad, you should have heard him! He was making demands and ordering me around like I was one of his flunkies," she complained. "And get this— he said if I don't go on the air and apologize, he's going to sue me."

"Tell him to bring it on! I'm not scared of him!"

A giggle fell out of her lips. "Dad, you can't fight Demetri Morretti—"

"I will if he disrespects you again."

"Don't worry, Dad. I can handle him."

"Baby girl, he's a bully. You can't take him on by yourself."

"I won't." Angela thought for a moment and considered what she could do to make the whole ugly issue with Demetri Morretti go away. "I'm thinking maybe I should ask the station to cancel the last segment of my *Athletes Behaving Badly* story."

"Why? I've watched all of the shows online, and I think it's one of the best pieces you've ever done."

"You think so?" she asked, stunned by her father's words. "You don't think I was too hard on the athletes featured in my story?"

"Hell no! They're all rich, spoiled stars who've had multiple run-ins with the law."

"Well, everyone except Demetri Morretti."

"Yeah, but he's the worst of the bunch. Talk about an overpaid, overhyped star. He had a lousy season, both on and off the field. If I was the GM of the Royals, I'd cut him loose."

"A lot of people feel that way."

"And for good reason. Remember the last home game we went to? Fans were so pissed, they started tossing things onto the field and screaming obscenities."

Frowning, Angela thought back to that day. She didn't remember any of that happening. But at the time, she imagined that she would've been too busy eyeballing Demetri Morretti to realize what was going on around her. In the midst of developing her *Athletes Behaving Badly* segment, she'd decided to use the time to scope out the players featured in her story. But when the stadium announcer called Demetri to bat, Angela ditched her iPad. There was something about the baseball star that excited her, something about his energy that turned her on. Her dad was sitting next to her, chatting away, but Angela hadn't heard a word he'd said.

Her eyes had been glued to number seven.

Demetri's uniform was crisp and clean and outlined his ripped forearms and firm butt. He had universal sex appeal, and when he took to the field, the women in the crowd went wild. Sitting there, in her plastic red seat, Angela felt something stir inside her. Something profound. Her attraction to him was so intense, it consumed her entire body.

Angela shook off the memories of that blustery fall day in September. *I'm attracted to Demetri—so what?* she decided. *I'm attracted to a lot of men, and just because I've fantasized about him a time or two doesn't mean I want him. Because I definitely don't.*

"Stay away from Demetri Morretti," Cornelius advised. "He's always been a loose cannon, and since injuring his shoulder during training camp, he's only gotten more volatile. There's no telling what he'll do the next time you two cross paths."

"Relax, Dad. He's not *that* bad."

"I just want you to be safe."

Angela smiled to herself. It didn't matter how many people online bashed her show. She would always have her dad's love and that meant the world to her. "I know, Dad, and don't worry. I will be."

"While I have you on the line, there's something else I'd like to discuss with you."

"Let me guess—you want me to get you some more Harlem Globetrotter tickets, right?"

"No, the ones you gave me last week were more than enough."

Angela heard her dad pause, then release a deep sigh, and immediately knew something was weighing heavily on his mind.

"Your brother called today."

"From where?" she quipped, rolling her eyes. "The Cook County Correctional Center?"

"Angela, don't joke about things like that."

"Why not? That's exactly where Rodney and his gang-banger friends are headed."

"This thing between you and your brother has gone on long enough," Cornelius said. "When are you going to forgive him and move on?"

"Dad, I moved on a long time ago."

"Then why won't you take his calls or respond to his messages?"

Because I've washed my hands of him. Angela didn't want to hurt her dad, and if she spoke the truth, he'd be crushed. "Dad, every time I think about what Rodney did to me, I get angry all over again, so let's talk about something else."

"No one's perfect, Angela. Everyone makes mistakes!"

"I know," she conceded, "but Rodney's mistakes always end up costing me thousands of dollars and a trip to the county jail to bail him out."

"He's only twenty-one. He has a lot of growing up to do—"

"Dad, quit making excuses for him. When I was in college and my scholarship fell through, I didn't go out and steal from my family. I got a job and worked damn hard." Angela felt a pang of guilt but pushed past it. Her dad didn't need to know the truth about the job she'd taken her freshman year. No one did. It was her little secret—one she was taking with her to her grave. "I busted my butt to make my dreams come true, and so can Rodney."

"I'm not condoning what your brother did, but I think

you're being too hard on him. He's the only brother you have, your flesh and blood, and he needs you now more than…"

Angela didn't have the strength to argue with her dad. Not after the day she'd had. And not about her wayward sibling, Rodney. Her brother was a full-time criminal who could outsmart the cops any day of the week. Over the years, she'd become accustomed to making excuses for his poor choices. But when he'd stolen her debit card and withdrawn five thousand dollars from her account, she'd cut him off for good. Angela missed having her kid brother around, missed shooting hoops with him in her dad's backyard and firing up the grill, but she'd never forgive Rodney for betraying her. "Dad, I'm tired," she said, anxious to end the phone call. "I'm going to turn in."

"Okay, I understand. You've had a long day."

"I'll talk to you tomorrow."

"Angela, please give some thought to what I said."

"I will," she lied. As she clicked off the phone and rose from the couch, she decided to put her problems with Rodney out of her mind. She had an interview with Demetri Morretti to prep for, and after their argument yesterday morning at Samson's Gym, Angela knew she had her work cut out for her.

After taking a quick shower, Angela got into bed, turned on her laptop and logged on to the internet. Once she checked her email and updated her Facebook page, she began typing "safe" interview questions. Questions she planned to submit to her boss but had no intention of asking Demetri Morretti on the air.

Excitement pumped through her veins. It didn't matter if they taped the episode next week or next month, because when the time finally came for her to sit down with the reigning bad boy of Major League Baseball, she'd not only have the upper hand, but she'd also be laying the groundwork for a promotion.

By the time I'm done with Demetri Morretti, he won't know what hit him!

Chapter 7

"Hold the elevator!"

Angela stuck her foot out to prevent the elevator doors from closing, and when Salem rounded the corner and hustled inside, she couldn't help but laugh. "The one time I decide to sneak out early, I get caught! Talk about rotten luck!"

Salem laughed, too. "Where are you rushing off to? Got a hot date tonight?"

"Nope, I'm getting a mani-pedi done up the block at Glamour Girlz."

"Mind if I join you? My gel nails are a hot mess."

"Sure. Why not? We can finally finish discussing my proposal."

"*Or,*" she said, drawing out the word, "we can gossip about our coworkers!"

Twenty minutes later, Angela and Salem were sitting in the café adjacent to Glamour Girlz. Since the salon was packed, and there was an hour-long wait, Angela suggested they grab a cup of coffee to pass the time. They were the only people in the café, and once seated at a corner table, Salem sank down in her padded leather chair and kicked off her pumps.

"God, I've been wanting to do that all day," she confessed, shrugging off her black two-button blazer. "Those shoes were cutting off my circulation."

Angela glanced under the table and gazed longingly at the multicolored peep-toe heels. She'd been coveting them for months, and had the perfect dress to wear them with, but because Rodney had pilfered her bank account, she wouldn't be making any trips to the mall anytime soon. "Those shoes are hot."

"I know, huh? I love my Louboutins, but after giving several studio tours, and running around the station all day, my feet are on fire!"

"I've been there too many times to count." Angela wore a sympathetic smile. "Sometimes it sucks to be a woman."

"Says the young, gorgeous newscaster who has men lining up to date her."

"Yeah," Angela conceded, rolling her eyes to the ceiling. "Broke, lazy types who want me to be their sugar mama!"

The women laughed.

Crossing her legs, Angela picked up a menu and scanned the day's specials. The Espresso Bar was a quaint spot with oak tables, fake flowers and framed paintings that looked as if they'd been done by three-year-olds. But Angela didn't come to the café to admire the decor; she came for the desserts. The Polish-born chef made the best pastries in the city. Cakes so rich and creamy, patrons ordered them for breakfast. When the waiter arrived to take their order, Angela felt no guilt in ordering a slice of chocolate *sformato* to go along with her cappuccino. She needed something sweet to give her fuel for the rest of the day.

"I might have to skip that manicure," Salem said, tapping the face of her watch. "It's getting late, and I have plans with my husband tonight."

"Are you guys going to the Cadillac Palace?" Angela wasn't a fan of the theater, but she loved connecting with viewers, and opening night of *Les Misérables* was sure to be a star-studded affair. "I'll be there with the crew, covering the event, and I think fans of *Eye on Chicago* are going to love getting an up-close view of what happens backstage."

"I really want to go, but my husband got tickets for the Vultures game."

"But you hate hockey."

"Yeah, but he loves it. And if I want him to go with me to the Enrique Iglesias concert next month, I have to suck it up and go cheer on the home team."

Turning her face toward the window, Angela touched a hand to her mouth and patted back a yawn. "Excuse me."

"Late night?"

"No, early morning." Swallowing another yawn, she dabbed her teary eyes with her fingertips and smiled sheepishly at her boss. "I had another session with my trainer this morning, and he worked me so hard, I hurt in places you wouldn't imagine!"

"Well, keep it up because all your hard work is paying off. Hey, think your trainer can whip me into shape? I'd love to drop a few pounds by my fortieth birthday."

Angela made a sour face. "Salem, you don't need to lose a single pound. I have handbags that weigh more than you!"

The waiter arrived and, after unloading the food from his tray, bowed chivalrously at the waist. "Enjoy your desserts, ladies. If you need anything else, don't hesitate to ask."

Angela watched Salem slice into her raspberry cheesecake and giggled when her boss moaned out loud. *Now's the perfect time to talk to Salem about my new proposal,* she decided, sipping her coffee. *She's high on sugar and caffeine—there's no way she'll blow me off!*

"I really enjoyed reading the proposal you turned in last week."

Inwardly, Angela cheered, but outwardly she remained as calm. "You did?"

"Yup, all nineteen pages!" A grin spread across her face. "One of these days, we're going to have to sit down and discuss a shorter, more succinct approach, though."

"I'm just glad you liked it. I worked on it for weeks."

"I know. It showed." Salem reached for her mug and took a sip of her chamomile tea. "You always do a great job on your proposals, but you really outdid yourself this time. Once

I started reading, I couldn't stop. Your report was *that* compelling."

Angela felt as if she were going to burst. Happiness filled her, and she was so overcome with excitement that she wanted to reach across the table and hug her boss. "Salem, thank you so much. I really appreciate this opportunity and I promise not to let you down."

Salem coughed, then pushed a hand through her long, wavy locks.

"I can't wait to get started. Would it be okay if we met tomorrow morning to discuss—"

"Angela, your proposal was outstanding, and the sexual harassment of female soldiers in the military is a story that needs to be told, but I can't approve it."

"Why not?" The question shot out of Angela's mouth before she could stop it. "I don't understand. You just said you loved my proposal."

"I do, but the story's all wrong for *Eye on Chicago.*"

"But the victims are Chicago natives and decorated war veterans, as well."

"I'm not trying to hurt your feelings, Angela, but viewers don't give a rat's behind about human-interest stories," she said with a shrug of her shoulders. "These days, all people care about is which celebrities are dating and who was caught with his pants down—*literally.*"

Plastering a smile on her face, one she hoped concealed her profound disappointment, Angela stirred her spoon furiously around her coffee mug.

"Online celebrity videos get millions of hits every day, but human-interest stories get little to no press," she continued, her expression contrite. "This is the first time *Eye on Chicago* has been number one in the ratings, and if we want to stay on top, we have to keep giving the viewers what they want."

"And what's that?"

"Scandalous, salacious stories featuring their favorite entertainers. People like…"

Angela sat frozen, with her eyes lowered and her lips pursed, listening to Salem go on and on about hot topics and future celebrity guests. She heard her cell phone buzz but didn't dare take her BlackBerry out of her purse. Although Angela was angry that Salem had shot down her proposal, reading her messages right then would be rude.

"Viewers have an insatiable appetite for celebrity gossip, and whenever you interview a ditzy actress or troubled athlete, fans tune in by the tens of thousands."

"I know," Angela agreed, "but we've been doing essentially the same show for the last nine months. I think it's time we shake things up and—"

"Hold that thought." Salem whipped her iPhone out of her jacket pocket and checked the screen. "This will only take a minute."

"No problem. Take as long as you need."

"Hello, Salem Velasquez speaking," she said, pressing her phone to her ear. Pushing away from the table, she hopped to her feet and strode toward the ladies' room.

Angela looked down at her dessert and pushed the plate aside. She didn't feel like eating. And if she thought her boss would understand, she'd grab her stuff and head home.

Staring aimlessly out the window, Angela watched as pedestrians drifted up and down the street. A guy wearing a Chicago Royals jersey and tattered jeans stood at the bus stop smoking a cigarette. The number seven was marked on the bottom of the shirt, and the initials *DM* were on each capped sleeve.

Those initials, of course, belonged to Demetri Morretti, the face of Grey Goose, Nike and a dozen other international companies. These days Angela couldn't go anywhere without seeing his handsome face splashed across a billboard, the side of a bus or a glossy magazine.

Her thoughts returned to last Friday and the exact moment she spotted Demetri Morretti at Samson's gym. Time stopped when their eyes met. Angela had been so stunned to see him that she had become hot and flustered. She'd dated a lot of men over the years but she'd never felt a spark with anyone. Never experienced that indescribable magic she saw in movies or read in romance novels. But every time she saw Demetri Morretti, Angela felt as if she was going to pass out. The man made her quiver. And tingle in the most delicious places. And that was reason enough for her to stay far away from him.

"Sorry I took so long." Salem plopped back down in her seat and rested her cell phone on the table. "That was Demetri Morretti's publicist, Nichola Caruso."

Angela's stomach lurched. She already knew what this was about and quickly racked her brain for a way out. She thought of telling her boss about her run-in with Demetri at the gym but decided against it. Salem would want to know details, and Angela didn't feel like rehashing her ten-minute conversation with the surly baseball star.

"I've got bad news," Salem said. "Morretti refuses to do your show."

Relief flowed through her. Angela wanted to scream for joy but kept her feelings to herself. Angela didn't want to look like a fool in front of her crew or her viewers and was secretly thrilled that the baseballer had turned Salem's offer down.

"You know what this means, right? He'll probably go ahead and sue us."

"I doubt it. Morretti's all talk." Angela wasn't scared of being sued, and she'd read online that defamation lawsuits were likely to be dismissed.

"You're probably right. It's not the first time someone's threatened to sue the station, and it won't be the last." Salem tapped her fingernails absently on the table. "I'm sure his legal team will talk him out of it. Suing us would be a waste of time and money."

Angela picked up her fork, sliced into her cake and tasted the dessert. Her head tilted to the side as she savored the moist, rich flavor. A smile tickled her lips. All wasn't lost. This wasn't over. One way or another, she'd find a way to convince Salem to approve her proposal. She had to. Her future was riding on it.

"I'm more upset about him not doing the interview than anything."

Angela gave a dismissive shrug of her shoulder and took another bite of her cake. "You win some, you lose some, I guess."

"This isn't over," Salem announced. "We're going to get Demetri on *Eye on Chicago* if it's the last thing we do."

"We? Count me out. I couldn't care less…" Catching the surprised look that crossed her boss's face, Angela broke off speaking and cleared her throat. "What I meant was, we've had really great guests this year, celebrities who actually *like* giving interviews, so why even bother with someone as grouchy as Demetri Morretti?"

"Because he's the hottest thing in sports right now!"

Attempting to play dumb, Angela made her eyes big and wide. "You think so?"

"Uh, yeah. Where have you been?"

Busy writing proposals no one gives a damn about, Angela thought, stabbing her cake with her fork. Were her colleagues right? Had she been hired because of her looks and not because of her talent? The truth weighed heavily on her, but before she could get Salem's take, her boss dropped another bombshell.

"Talk to Demetri tonight when you see him at Dolce Vita. And by 'talk,' I mean do whatever it takes to get him on your show."

Angela stared openmouthed at her frizzy-haired boss.

"Get him alone, away from his entourage, and work that Angela Kelly charm," she advised. "And this time, no yelling or screaming at him, okay?"

Angela's cheeks burned like fire. Ever since her argument with Demetri went viral, everyone from the cameramen to the engineers had been teasing her. Salem thought the video was great press and had even spoken to their computer tech about uploading the clip to the station website. But Angela was dead set against it and had talked the tech guy out of posting it.

"We have to strike while the iron's hot, and since your showdown with Demetri, the whole city's been buzzing about you *and* your show."

"How do you know Demetri will be at Dolce Vita tonight?" Angela asked. "The guy's a recluse who rarely goes to parties or local events anymore. And when he does, he never stays more than ten or fifteen minutes."

"Dolce Vita is his brother Nicco's brainchild, and Demetri has attended restaurant openings from Tokyo to Dubai." Salem looked determined. "Angela, I want Demetri Morretti on *Eye on Chicago* during sweeps week—"

"Then why don't *you* talk to him?" Angela heard the edge in her voice and rephrased the question. "You're the producer of the show, and if you called him up and talked to him about an appearance, it would carry more weight."

"I would, but Demetri's not sweet on me. He's sweet on *you.*"

"No, he's not. He hates my guts, and the feeling's definitely mutual."

"*Hate* is a strong word," Salem said, raising her eyebrows. "Especially for two people who have insane chemistry like you guys do."

"Chemistry?" Angela shook her head and the thought clear out of her mind. "You must be confusing us, because the only thing Demetri Morretti and I have in common is mutual disgust and animosity for one another."

"There's a thin line between love and hate…" she sing-songed. "And trust me, when it comes to you and Demetri Morretti, the lines have already blurred."

"No, they're not. I know exactly where I stand. He's not my type, I'm not even remotely attracted to him, and to be honest, I think he's obnoxious."

"Oh, drop the act already! You're not fooling anybody, Angela."

"What act?" Angela fussed with the silver necklace draped in front of her purple V-neck sweater. "I don't know what you're talking about."

"Sure you don't." Salem studied her closely and then wagged an index finger at her. "Just admit it. You're attracted to Demetri Morretti, just like every other woman in America. Hell, the man gives me butterflies, too, and I'm a newlywed!"

Angela had zero interest in talking to Demetri again, but she couldn't dismiss her boss. Not after all Salem had done for her. They were friends, the only two women of color at WJN-TV. And Angela could always count on her producer to go to bat for her. But that didn't mean she was willing to throw herself at Demetri Morretti. There were just some things Angela couldn't do, and begging him to appear on her show was one of them.

"Salem, I'll do anything to make *Eye on Chicago* a success, but I'm not a miracle worker. Demetri isn't going to talk to me, let alone agree to be on my show."

"I think he will." Her smile was coy. "His personal chef is in my yoga class, and yesterday she mentioned that Demetri's foundation is having a Fourth of July extravaganza for hundreds of children and their families."

"Okay," Angela said, slowly drawing out the word.

"Maybe if you agree to cover the event, he'll agree to do your show."

Angela wished she shared her boss's optimism, but she didn't. "I doubt it."

"Then try talking to his publicist, Nichola Caruso," Salem said while signaling the waiter for the check. "There are rumors circulating that they're lovers, and apparently, she can persuade Demetri to do anything."

"I bet." Angela had heard the rumors about Demetri and his publicist and didn't doubt for a second they were true. She'd seen pictures of them eating at five-star restaurants, shopping on the Magnificent Mile and cruising around in one of his many sports cars. Athletes got a kick out of sleeping with their staff, and the internet was saturated with intimate photographs of Demetri and his female employees. "I'm not trying to be difficult, Salem, but how do you expect me to persuade Demetri to be on my show when he obviously doesn't want to?"

Salem winked. "You're a smart girl. You'll think of something."

"That's just it. I don't think I can!"

"You do want *Eye on Chicago* to stay on top of the ratings, right?"

"Yes, of course, but—"

"Good," she said curtly. "Then quit arguing and go get me that interview."

Chapter 8

Touted as the hottest restaurant lounge in the city, Dolce Vita Chicago offered world-class food. Its stylish rooms were draped in plush black silk, and its terrace was decked out in cozy furniture, vanilla-scented candles and hanging lights that bathed the space in a soft blue light.

"Let's head upstairs," Angela suggested, addressing her three-man crew. The restaurant was crowded, packed from wall to wall with Chicago's brightest stars. The air was saturated with the scent of expensive perfume and fine Italian cuisine. "I spotted a famous blogger head into the VIP area, and I'd love to get him on camera. He always has something outrageous to say!"

"My lower back is killing me," the cameraman complained, sliding the camera off his shoulder and resting it at his side. "I need a break."

"Another one?" Angela glanced at her thin silver watch. "But it's only been thirty minutes since your *last* break."

The lighting technician spoke up. "Yeah, but we put in four long hours at the Cadillac Palace, and the music was so loud, it gave me a headache."

Angela smelled alcohol on his breath and knew his last bathroom break had involved a trip to the bar. She had warned him not to drink on the job, but instead of calling him out in front of the rest of the crew, she reached for the Tylenol inside her purse. "Want some?" she asked, presenting the bottle in her hand.

Shaking his head, he stared down at his sneaker-clad feet.

"I need a five, too." The sound assistant took a pack of cigarettes out of his pocket. "Climbing up and down those steps holding our equipment was no walk in the park, Angela."

I managed just fine, she thought, nixing an eye roll. *And I'm wearing stilettos!* "Let's go strong for the next hour and then finish up. Once we get some shots from the roof and I do another quick round of interviews, we can call it a night."

"Or we can call it a night now." The cameraman wore a grin. "It'll be our little secret."

Angela shot him down. "No way. We have takes to redo, and—"

"We're not redoing any shots, Angela. I told you, everything looks fine."

"'Fine' isn't good enough, Mac. The footage needs to be perfect, and those clips we shot earlier aren't fit to air," she told him, refusing to back down.

"I don't have the energy to refilm." The cameraman opened his mouth wide and yawned so loud, he startled a couple standing nearby. "Are you forgetting that we put in a full eight-hour shift today at the station?"

Angela didn't like his condescending tone, but she didn't lose her cool. "I've been up since four-thirty this morning, but you don't hear me complaining."

"Yeah, getting gussied up in hair and makeup is *real* tiring work." Snickering, the cameraman bumped elbows with his colleagues. "Anytime you want to swap jobs, let me know!"

"One interview and then we'll take another quick break."

"Break first, interview second." The lighting technician watched a buxom waitress sashay by and licked his thin chapped lips. "I'm going to the bar. I need some, ah, water."

Angela crossed her arms. This was why she hated working with this crew. They complained about everything, took countless breaks and had the attention span of a toddler in a toy store. "Ten minutes, guys. That's it."

Their eyes lit up with boyish excitement.

"Let's meet in the lobby at…" Angela paused to glance down at her watch, but when she looked up, her crew was gone. Peering around the lounge, she watched the trio make themselves at home at the sleek circular bar.

"There you are! We've been looking all over for you!"

At the sound of her girlfriend's high-pitched voice, Angela spun around. Her friends Remy Foster and Farrah Washington were dressed to kill in short, flirty dresses and wearing huge matching smiles. "I'm so glad you guys could make it!" Angela said, throwing her arms around them. "It's been forever since we hung out."

"Who you tellin'? It's been so long, I forgot what you looked like!" Remy joked. "Let's go grab a booth. I need some champagne."

Angela raised an eyebrow. "Champagne? Why? What are we celebrating?"

"The fact that we're the sexiest chicks in here!" Striking a model pose, Remy raised her chin and slid her bejeweled hands up and down her thick, voluptuous shape. "I'm killing them in this dress. Every guy in here is checking me out, *especially* the married ones!"

Laughing, the three friends linked arms. A waiter arrived, and as he escorted them through the dining area, Angela spotted several famous faces partying in Dolce Vita. A Grammy Award–winning rock group and a movie icon and her latest boy toy were seated on a black velvet couch, posing for pictures and downing body shots.

"Can I start you gorgeous ladies off with something from the bar?" the waiter asked, his head cocked and his pen poised to write on his notepad. "Some cocktails, maybe?"

"For sure!" Remy picked up a menu and scanned it. "We'll have a round of peach Bellinis and an appetizer basket with a double order of calamari."

"Coming right up!" The waiter nodded and then ran off.

"I wonder what's keeping Simone?" Farrah took her cell phone out of her purse. "I expected her to be here by now. She's always on time."

"Simone's not coming," Angela said absently, scanning the bar for her camera crew. They were nowhere to be found, but Angela hoped when she was ready to resume filming, they'd be ready to work.

"Are Jayden and Jordan okay?" Farrah wore a concerned face. "They didn't catch that nasty stomach bug that's been going around, did they?"

Shaking her head, Angela abandoned her search for her crew. "No, the boys are fine. Marcus whisked Simone away to St. Bart's for the weekend, and trust me, ladies, the girl's on cloud nine!" Angela laughed. "She called a couple hours ago to let me know they arrived safely *and* to brag about sitting next to Hugh Jackman in first class."

Farrah snorted. "Why are we friends with her again?"

"Because she's one hell of a cook!" Remy hollered. Throwing her arms around her girlfriends, she hoisted her cell phone in the air and shrieked, "Say 'cheese'!"

Remy snapped picture after picture and then uploaded the images on her Facebook and Twitter accounts.

"Remy, do you have to do that now?" Farrah asked, raising her voice above the noise in the dining room. "We came down here to have a good time, not to watch you play on your phone all night."

"Of course I have to load the pictures now. I want all my friends *and* frenemies to see how much fun I'm having at Dolce Vita!"

Three waiters, carrying trays topped with enough food to feed a family of ten, swiftly entered the dining room. Stopping in front of the booth, they unloaded their trays on the raised mahogany table. "This isn't our order," Angela said, waving her hands out in front of her. "We ordered a round of Bellinis and an appetizer basket. That's it."

"Shhh, girl." Putting an index finger to her crimson-red lips, Remy jabbed Angela in the side with her elbow. "Don't say anything. We're about to get free food."

"This is courtesy of Demetri Morretti," the blue-eyed waiter said. "After you finish eating dinner, he'd like you and your friends to join him in the VIP lounge."

"Tell him we'll be there in ten minutes." Remy grabbed a champagne flute and giggled. "Thanks, fellas. Everything looks delish!"

A fourth waiter arrived, carrying the largest bouquet of yellow tulips Angela had ever seen, and he handed it to her. "These are for you, Ms. Kelly."

Angela sat there, dumbfounded. She couldn't think or speak and was glad Farrah had the presence of mind to thank the waiters and give them a generous tip.

"Thank you," the headwaiter said. "We'll be back shortly with the second course."

Farrah frowned. "The second course? Just how many courses are there?"

"Seven," the waiters said in unison.

"Wonderful! Thanks, guys!" Remy said, shooting them a wink. "Hurry back!"

"Wow, look at all this food," Farrah gushed, her eyes big and wide. "And there's still more to come. Demetri Morretti must *really* like you."

Remy shrieked. "Girl, you better go up to the VIP lounge and give him some! Hot, rich guys are hard to find, and if I were you, I'd do Demetri Morretti and *do him well!*"

Her friends erupted in laughter.

"Aren't you going to read the card?" Farrah asked, pointing at the bouquet.

Angela's face flushed and her body stiffened. She then plucked the tiny white card out of the lavish bouquet. "'To the most beautiful woman in the room,'" she read out loud, as if puzzled over the words. And she was. The last time she had seen Demetri they'd argued, and now, less than a week later, he was sending her yellow tulips. Her favorite flower. "'I look forward to spending the rest of the night with you and your gorgeous friends.'"

"I thought you and Demetri hated each other?"

Angela stumbled over her words. "W-we do."

"Then why did he send over flowers, dinner and three bottles of Cristal?"

"I don't know, Farrah. Maybe he gets off on being insulted."

"There's gotta be more to this story than you're telling us," Remy insisted. "You had wild, passionate sex with Demetri in your office, didn't you?"

"Of course not! I'd never do something like that."

Remy hollered, "I would!"

"Come on," Farrah pleaded. "Tell us what's really going on between you and that gorgeous man. We're your girls, remember?"

As they ate, Angela told her girlfriends about what had happened with Demetri at Samson's Gym and her conversation at the Espresso Bar with her boss. "Salem practically ordered me to speak to him tonight," she said, staring down at the flower bouquet. "I wasn't going to, but now it looks like I have to. Demetri's obviously in a good mood, so I'm going to see if I can get him to reconsider the interview."

"What are you going to do if he shoots you down again?"

"He won't turn her down," Remy said. "Angela's got this in the bag."

Farrah glanced up from her plate. "Wow, you sound confident. What makes you so sure she'll convince him to do her show?"

"Because once this chick gets an idea in her mind, there's just no stopping her!"

"That's true," Farrah agreed.

Overcome with confusion, Angela sat there, trying to figure out what Demetri Morretti was up to. This had to be yet another sophisticated ploy to deceive her. Or was it? Could the flowers have been a generous peace offering and nothing more? She shook her head, quickly pushing the later thought from her mind.

Lowering her face into the bouquet, Angela closed her eyes and inhaled the sweet, fragrant scent. Angela loved flowers and was a sucker for elaborate romantic gestures. This was easily the nicest thing anyone had ever done for her. Dolce Vita was overrun with celebrities—rich, glamorous types whom legions of people envied—but she was the only woman who'd received flowers. And even more shocking, they were from a man who hated her!

"Are you still in a funk because that TV newscaster dissed you on her show?"

Demetri didn't have to look over his shoulder to know his brothers were behind him. He was standing in front of the oversize window in the VIP room, surveying the scene down below, when Nicco and Rafael sidled up beside him. They stood well over six feet tall, both with a full head of wavy black hair. Dressed in their casual white suits, they could easily pass for Hugo Boss models.

Nicco and Rafael were always ribbing him because he was the youngest, but tonight Demetri wasn't in the mood for their teasing. "No, I'm straight. Forgot all about it."

"Then why are you over here crying in your drink?" Nicco broke into a hearty chuckle. "You look pitiful, bro, and you're bringing down the mood in my bar. Get it together, man. Crying is bad for business!"

"Shut up, Nicco. You don't see me cracking on you for crashing your Maserati *again*."

He shrugged his shoulders. "Hey, man, accidents happen."

Rafael wore a coy grin. "Maybe next time you'll keep your hands on the wheel and *off* your girlfriend's double Ds."

"What girlfriend? I'm single."

"What happened to the Playboy Bunny from Nepal?" Demetri asked.

"She dumped me. Said I had trust issues."

"She's right! You do!" Rafael and Demetri shouted in unison.

"We're not talking about me. We're talking about you." Nicco pointed a finger at Demetri. "You need to chill out and quit stressing. Who cares what the media says about you?"

"I do. I'm sick of people dogging me out."

"I'm not surprised. You've always been sensitive."

Demetri raised his chin and straightened his bent shoulders. "I'm not sensitive."

"Yeah, you are," Rafael insisted with a curt nod of his head. "You're the sensitive one, Nicco's the stubborn one, and I'm the cool, laid-back one who keeps you both in check."

The brothers chuckled.

"Want me to talk to this Angela Kelly woman for you?" Nicco asked, hiding a self-incriminating grin. "I'll tell her to quit bad-mouthing you on her show, and if that doesn't work, I'll storm into her studio, and… Oh, wait, you already did that!"

Rafael playfully slapped Demetri's shoulder. "Ignore him, D. I saw Angela Kelly in the lobby a few minutes ago, and she's a stunner. If she had gone off on me like that, I'd be crying, too!"

"She's here? Are you sure?" Nicco asked, glancing wildly around the VIP room. "I personally thanked all the members of the media for coming tonight, but I definitely didn't run across anyone from WJN-TV."

Rafael slowly swept his gaze through the main-floor bar and lounge. "There she is! In the corner booth across from the kitchen."

"I hope you never witness a crime, because you'd suck at describing the perp!" Nicco gestured to the crowd with his glass. "Could you be a little more descriptive? There are dozens of beauties in the lounge, and I still don't have a clue who she is."

"Five-nine. Honey-brown skin. Killer curves." Demetri's hungry gaze slid down Angela's trim, fit body. "Little black dress. Gold accessories. Nude pumps."

"Damn, bro, can you see what's *under* her dress, too?"

The brothers erupted in laughter.

"Now I see why you're bummed," Nicco said with a frown. "Angela Kelly's gorgeous, easily the sexiest woman in here tonight."

I know, and I can't get her out of my mind! Demetri dragged a hand over his face. Since their run-in last week at the gym, he'd thought about Angela nonstop. After arriving home, he had called his publicist and ordered her to delete her blog post about Angela. He then spent the rest of the afternoon watching old episodes of *Eye on Chicago* online. The more he watched, the more intrigued he was about the fresh-faced beauty. And reading her online blog had given him an idea. When the waiter presented her with the lavish flower bouquet, her face lit up, and Demetri knew he was one step closer to earning her forgiveness.

"I'll be right back," Nicco said, adjusting his collar. "Since I'm the owner of this fine establishment, I'm going downstairs to introduce myself to Angela Kelly."

"I bet that's not all you're going to do," Demetri grumbled. The thought of his brother stepping to Angela made his temperature rise. He didn't want anyone, especially a smooth talker like Nicco, putting the moves on Angela. Not when he was trying to make peace with her.

That's not all you're trying to do, jeered his inner voice.

"Be careful," Rafael warned. "If you piss her off she'll crucify you on her show!"

Nicco gave a hearty chuckle. "I know. That's why I'm

going to welcome her to Dolce Vita and tell the waiters to give her the star treatment."

Rafael cocked an eyebrow. "And get her number, too, right?"

"A man can never have too many beautiful women in his life…"

"Hey, guys!" Nichola said, her smile bright and her tone filled with enthusiasm.

Rafael gave her a one-arm hug. "Are you having a good time or is this guy making you work the room?"

"I'm having a blast. The lounge is packed with celebrities and the food is crazy-good!" Nichola pointed a finger at the bar. "Demetri, I need you to do a quick interview with the guy from *Sports Chicago*. He's been waiting to talk to you for the last hour, and he's starting to get antsy."

"Go do your interview," Nicco said. "I have some business to attend to anyways."

"We'll hook up later, bro!"

His brothers strode off, leaving Demetri alone with his publicist. Demetri didn't want to talk to the guy from *Sports Chicago* or any other press about his shoulder injury. Not tonight. He wanted to hang out with his friends and talk to Angela Kelly—alone, in private. At the thought of her, he sneaked a glance over his shoulder. He watched Angela exit her booth, with her girlfriends in tow, and wondered where she was rushing off to. Sailing through the lounge, the gorgeous trio left a trail of mesmerized, wide-eyed men in their wake.

"If you do this interview, I won't bother you for the rest of the night."

He raised an eyebrow. "Promise?"

"Don't be silly. I can't do that!" Giggling, she waved off his comment with a flick of her hand. "It's my job to keep your name in the press and get you free publicity, remember?"

"I know. I know. That's what you keep telling me." Removing the cap on his water bottle, Demetri nodded at the portly reporter, sitting alone at the end of the bar. "Let's get this over and done with so I can get back to having fun."

"That's the spirit! Let's give a great interview and land a cover story!"

Chapter 9

"I can't find them anywhere!" Arms folded, her teeth clenched in suppressed rage, Angela searched frantically around the lounge, hoping to find her crew among the well-heeled diners. She wondered if the lead anchor had a hand in this. The lead anchor, a distinguished older man with refined mannerisms, was always trying to embarrass her, and this was just the sort of thing he'd put the guys up to. "How am I supposed to interview the season-two winner of *The Song* if I don't have a cameraman?"

"We're wasting precious time," Remy complained, tapping one of her sandal-clad feet impatiently on the floor. "Time we *should* be spending in the VIP lounge partying with Demetri Morretti and his rich baller friends."

"I'm not here to party, Remy. I'm here to work."

"But your crew bailed on you! As I see it, you're done for the night."

Angela took her cell phone out of her purse. She didn't want to bother Salem on her night off, but her boss had a right to know what was going on. Angela dialed her number and it went to voice mail. She left a message and then searched the dance floor for any signs of her crew.

"I didn't get dolled up to stand around doing nothing," Remy complained. "I'm going to the VIP lounge to meet some men. Are you coming or not?"

Angela couldn't help but laugh. There was never a dull moment when the man-crazed makeup artist was around.

When they reached the entrance of the VIP lounge and her friends squealed with joy, Angela cracked up. Guests were mingling, posing for pictures, and the blonde female DJ was forcing dancers into a gyrating frenzy. Two brunettes, wearing itty-bitty dresses and blinding smiles, stood at the door offering glasses of champagne and an eyeful of cleavage.

When Angela stepped inside the lounge, the first person she saw was Demetri Morretti. He looked handsome and cool. Like the kind of man she usually lusted after. It was the first time Angela had seen Demetri without his baseball cap on, and his short textured hair gave him a mature look. He was standing at the back of the room, chatting with his publicist and a slim man with a straggly ponytail.

Watching him, Angela decided that the editors at *J'* magazine were right. Demetri Morretti *was* the best-looking man on the planet. Hands down. None of the other men featured in the magazine even came close. He was immaculately groomed, and his casual white shirt, leather jacket and blue jeans fit his toned, ripped physique perfectly. He was fine in every sense of the word and had the sexiest set of lips Angela had ever seen. But his best feature was his eyes. They were dark, filled with intrigue and framed with long eyelashes. Demetri Morretti was a chick magnet, and Angela noticed everyone—from the pop singer to the mayor's daughter—blatantly check him out.

"Oh, my God! Nicco Morretti's here!" Remy grabbed Angela's forearm and gave it a hard squeeze. "Girl, you have to introduce me."

"Me?" Angela touched a hand to her chest. "Why me? I don't even know the guy."

"Yeah, but his younger brother is crushing on you, bad."

"Forget it, Remy. Every time I introduce you to someone, I end up regretting it."

"Come on. Be a good sport," she begged, her voice shrill. "You don't want to stand in the way of true love, do you?"

Farrah burst out laughing. "True love? Ten minutes ago,

you were dirty dancing with a Sony music producer, and now Nicco Morretti is your one true love?"

"Girl, you'd be in love, too, if you knew how much his net worth was!"

In her peripheral vision, Angela saw Demetri stride out of the lounge with his cell phone at his ear and a frown on his lips. Her eyes followed him out of the room and down the long, narrow hallway. He looked upset, but Angela wanted to speak to Demetri alone—without his entourage listening in—and knew this was her best chance to have some one-on-one time.

"Do you guys mind if I step outside for a minute?" Angela asked, her eyes glued to the window. "I need to speak to Demetri, but I won't be long. Ten, fifteen minutes, tops."

Remy smirked. "Don't hurry back on my account. There are more than enough ballers here to keep me busy!"

Angela found Demetri outside the VIP lounge, leaning against the far wall. His head was back, his eyes were closed, and his hands were hanging loosely at his sides. He was the picture of calm, and seeing him like this—all relaxed—made Angela wonder if she'd made a mistake following him out into the hall. Deciding she had, she spun around on her heels, anxious to return to the VIP lounge and her friends.

"I like your perfume."

At the sound of his voice, Angela turned and faced Demetri. He was standing in the middle of the hallway, staring right at her. Intently. Then, after a long, terse minute, he broke into a wide, disarming smile. One that put her on high alert.

"How was dinner?"

"Amazing," she gushed. "Thanks for everything. The flowers, the food, the champagne. Everything was delicious."

"I'm glad to hear it. Are we cool now?"

"That depends. Are you still planning to sue me?"

"I need you to stop dissing me on your show, Angela. It kills."

She waited for Demetri to chuckle or break out into a grin, but when he didn't, Angela knew he was serious. Dead serious. That stunned her. Demetri was a rich bad-boy athlete who settled disagreements with his fists, so why did he care what she thought of him? His sensitivity was endearing, a complete surprise, and Angela found herself even more intrigued by him.

"What's it going to take to squash this beef between us?" he asked.

"You could do my show."

"I don't do interviews."

"Why? Scared the questions will hit too close to home?"

"I'm not scared of anything." Demetri's gaze was as intense as the tone of his voice. He appeared stern, like a corporal, and spoke through clenched teeth. "I've been double-crossed too many times to count, and I don't have the stomach for lies and bullshit anymore."

Pausing reflectively, Angela took a moment to consider his words. "That's not what I'm about, Demetri. I'm not going to trick you or humiliate you on my show, but I will ask you tough questions. Questions my viewers are dying to know the answers to."

"So, if I come on your show you'll stop gunning for me?"

"I'm not gunning for you," she said, shaking her head.

"You called me an immature, overpaid athlete who cares more about winning bar brawls than a baseball championship."

Angela winced. Those weren't her words. Sure, they'd come out of her mouth, but her *Athletes Behaving Badly* piece had been tweaked, cut and rewritten by the producers. On the day of taping, she'd dutifully read the teleprompter and was so busy trying to nail the segment in the first take, she hadn't given a second thought to what she was reading. But Angela couldn't tell Demetri that. He wouldn't understand. Not after she'd criticized him for not writing his own blog.

"Maybe you're right. Maybe I was a bit harsh," she conceded, pinching two fingers together. "But if you come on my show, I'll give you the opportunity to set the record straight. That's forty commercial-free minutes to plug your endorsements, your charity and give a shout-out to your ten million followers on Twitter."

Demetri raised an eyebrow. "Ten million? Is that a lot?"

"Most athletes don't even have half that number, so I'd say you're doing okay."

"As long as I have more followers than my brothers I'm happy!"

They shared a laugh.

"Please reconsider doing my show," Angela said, hoping to capitalize on their truce.

"Fax the questions to my publicist, Nichola Caruso, and we'll look them over."

"No way. If we're going to do this, we're going to do it my way." Hearing the bite in her tone, she cleared her throat and took a moment to gather her thoughts. Convincing Demetri to come on her show was a daunting task, but Angela was up for the challenge. Every time Demetri smiled or stared deep into her eyes, her heart fluttered in her chest. "I want us to have an open, honest conversation, not a scripted interview with you and your team calling the shots."

"You're one tough cookie, Ms. Kelly."

"I'm a Chi-Town girl," she quipped. "What do you expect?"

Demetri shot her an amused look. "Can I have your number?"

"Why? So you can prank call my house?"

"No, so we can discuss this further," he explained, stepping forward and sliding his hands into his pockets. "Maybe we can get together tomorrow and iron out the details."

"I can't. I already have plans."

"With your boyfriend?"

"Don't have one. Don't need one," she singsonged. "I volunteer at the food bank on Saturdays. You should come. We could always use more volunteers."

"I just might."

"Sure you will."

"Why is that so hard to believe?"

"Because you're Demetri Morretti, baseball player extraordinaire," she said, raising her voice. "These days, celebrities don't do anything unless it's a planned photo op, and I hate to disappoint you, Demetri, but there won't be any fanfare at the food bank."

"Don't need any." He took his cell phone out of his jacket pocket and handed it to her. "Can you enter all of the necessary information in here?"

Angela knew Demetri wasn't going to show, but to humor him she took his cell phone and entered the details. They were on good terms—for now—and until he agreed to do her show, she was going to be on her best behavior. But once they taped the interview, all bets were off.

"I'll be there at nine o'clock."

Laughing, she slid his cell phone back into his front pocket. "I'll have to see it to believe it." Anxious to get back to her friends and away from the gorgeous baseball player, Angela spun around and waved a hand high in the air. "Good night, Demetri. Thanks again for dinner."

"Hold up."

Capturing her forearm in his palm, he slowly drew her toward him. Their faces were close, their bodies touching. The air was thick, saturated with the scent of his desire. His rich, refreshing cologne made Angela feel light on her feet.

"Not so fast, beautiful. We're not done talking."

Angela swallowed. Her mind was spinning, and her flesh was scalding hot. She didn't trust herself to speak, not with the way she was feeling inside, but managed to croak out a response. "I have to get back inside. My girlfriends are waiting for me."

"But you haven't given me your number yet." He drew his gaze from her lips to her eyes and ran a hand down the length of her arm. "How are we supposed to get to know each other if I have no way of reaching you?"

Angela stared at him openmouthed. *He's joking, right?*

Standing chest to chest with Demetri Morretti in the darkened hallway was asking for trouble. Angela knew it. Felt it. But she didn't move away. Not when her legs were shaking uncontrollably and her feet were glued to the floor. Angela started to speak but struggled with her words. His smile was so sweet and wild, outrageous thoughts attacked her mind. Scared Demetri was going to kiss her or worse, she stepped back. Right into the wall. Now she was stuck, trapped with nowhere to go and nowhere to hide.

How in the world did we get here? Angela wondered, licking her lips. A week ago, Demetri was plotting her demise, and now he looked as though he wanted to kiss her. More shocking still, she wanted to kiss him, too.

Checking her thoughts, she ordered her horny body to get under control. Nothing good could come out of fooling around with Demetri Morretti, and Angela wasn't willing to ruin her career or her reputation for one night of carnal pleasure.

"You have the perfect look for TV, you know."

Angela blinked. "I do?"

"You come alive in front of the camera." He spoke in a whisper, one that made shivers dance along her spine. "You have an incredibly sexy voice and perfect diction."

"Perfect diction?" A nervous giggle fell out of her mouth. "I've heard a lot of crazy pick-up lines over the years, but that one's a first."

"Pick-up lines are whack. I prefer to speak from the heart."

Her heart stood still when he touched her cheek. "What

would your publicist think if she knew you were out here flirting with me?"

Lines of confusion wrinkled his forehead. "It's none of her business."

"But you're lovers."

"I'm single. Have been for over a year."

"I saw a video of you guys on *Entertainment Tonight*," she said, unable to conceal the note of accusation in her voice. "You looked awfully cozy in Maui with her last week."

"Are you keeping tabs on me?"

Angela couldn't think of a witty comeback and knew if she spoke, her feelings would betray her, so shook her head instead.

"Nichola's like a sister to me. There's nothing going on between us."

"You're not friends with benefits?"

"I don't believe in that. Not my speed."

Angela threw her head back and let out a laugh. "Yeah, right! Athletes are the biggest players on the face of the earth, and when it comes to deceiving women, they have no conscience."

"I've never been a player. Now, my brother Nicco is a different story." A grin crimped his lips. "He loves chasing women and doesn't have a faithful bone in his entire body."

"And you do?"

"Most definitely."

"So, all those tabloid stories about you dating various Hollywood starlets are lies?"

"There's only one woman I'm feeling right now. She's a tenacious TV newscaster with bright, beautiful eyes and a gorgeous smile, but unfortunately, she thinks I'm a complete jerk." Demetri bent his head low and dropped his mouth to her ear. "Don't know if I can change her perception of me, but I'm going to try. Starting right now...."

Then Demetri covered her mouth with his lips.

Stunned, Angela felt her eyes widen and her breath catch in her throat. She couldn't describe the feelings that washed over her when their lips touched. The urgency and hunger of his kiss overwhelmed her. His caress was tender, his hands soft, and his lips were the best thing she'd ever had the pleasure of tasting. Using his tongue, he parted her lips and eagerly explored every inch of her mouth.

Loud, heavy footsteps reverberated around the corridor. A bulb flashed, flooding the hallway with a harsh, bright light. Pulling away from Demetri, Angela covered her face with her hands and turned her body toward the wall.

"Get out of here!" Demetri shouted, sliding in front of Angela. Shielding her with his body, he pointed a finger at the grizzly-haired photographer snapping pictures with his high-powered camera. "Scram, or I'll shove that camera down your throat!"

Two bouncers, in black muscle shirts and jeans, appeared at the end of the hallway and snatched the photographer up by his jacket collar. "This clown must have snuck up here through the bathroom window," one said. "Don't worry, Demetri. We'll take care of him."

The bouncers dragged the photographer into the elevator, and the doors slid closed.

"Angela, are you okay?

"Yeah, I'm fine." She touched a hand to her lips, to the exact place where Demetri had kissed her. His soft caress, along her bare arms, caught her off guard. Slowly, he turned her around. Her breath came in quick, shallow gulps. Not because she was scared but because she was overcome with desire and wanted nothing more to pick up where they'd left off.

"You're shaking." Demetri took off his jacket and draped it over her delicate shoulders. "Don't worry. Those pictures will never see the light of day. The bouncers will confiscate his camera, then toss him out into the back alley."

Angela released an audible sigh. "That's good to know."

"Let's head back inside. You look like you could use a drink."

"No, you go ahead. I need to use the ladies' room."

"Then I'll wait right here."

"Demetri, that's really not necessary."

"It is to me." A smile dimpled his cheeks. "Go on. I'll be patiently waiting right here."

As he watched Angela walk down the hall, his gaze slid along her hips and her long, toned legs. And when she slipped inside the ladies' room, he released a long, slow whistle. He couldn't believe it. He'd kissed Angela Kelly—the woman who'd slandered his name on national TV. He was so hungry for her, he wanted to call it a night and head back to his place. In a moment of weakness, his desire for the provocative newscaster had overruled his logic, and he'd acted on his impulse. Angela Kelly was a spitfire, a woman full of contradictions and surprises, and he was interested in learning more about her. A lot more.

He slumped against the wall and rubbed a hand over his face. He felt as if he'd been struck upside the head with a foul ball, and the more he tried to censor his feelings, the stronger his desire for Angela Kelly grew. His brain went into overdrive, entertaining one outrageous thought after another. Thoughts of sleeping with the enemy.

Now it's a whole new ball game, he decided, casting a glance at the ladies' room.

And that excited him.

Chapter 10

The Cook County Food Bank was a large brick building bordered by broken-down houses with rusted for-sale signs. When Angela pulled into the parking lot and saw the litter on the ground, she made a mental note to speak to the director about hiring someone from the Ninth Street shelter. The participants in her employment-readiness class were desperately looking for work, and one of them would do a good job keeping the area spick-and-span.

Exiting her car, she spotted Farrah on the other side of the lot and waved in greeting.

"Hey, girl," Farrah said, heaving her tote bag over her shoulder. "I wasn't expecting to see you until the afternoon."

"Why? I told you I'd be here bright and early."

"I know, but when I left Dolce Vita, you and Demetri were still going strong."

"We were talking, Farrah. Just talking," Angela stressed.

"More like gazing and flirting and touching!" Her eyes twinkled and her smile was tinged with amusement. "I saw you guys all hugged up on the couch. And at one point, Demetri was even holding your hand. Don't try and deny it. I saw it with my own eyes."

A smile appeared across Angela's mouth as the memory of last night played in her mind. Fast-forwarding past the interviews she'd done and the argument with her crew, she mused over the hot, tantalizing kiss she'd shared with Demetri—the one that had stolen her breath. It was two minutes of heaven, the most electrifying and passionate kiss she'd ever experienced. After returning to the VIP lounge, she'd sat with Demetri in a quiet corner, talking and laughing. At the end of the night, long after the restaurant had closed, he'd walked her to her car and given her another long, slow kiss. One that kindled her body's fire and unleashed her desires. But Angela couldn't tell her friend that. "My boss ordered me to get Demetri on my show, so I have to be nice to him until he signs on." To convince herself, and Farrah, she gave a shrug of her shoulders. "It was nothing."

"It sure *looked* like something."

Ignoring the dig, Angela followed Farrah up the rickety wooden steps.

"When are you seeing him again?"

"Hopefully, he'll agree to do my show, and we can tape the interview by the end of—"

"No one cares about your show," Farrah said, flapping a hand in the air. "I want to know when you and the sexiest man alive are going on your first official date."

"Farrah, it's not like that."

"Oh, yes, it is! You want Demetri so bad that lust is literally oozing from your pores!" Farrah's head cocked to the side, and she reached out and patted Angela's stomach. "Before you know it, you'll have a little bun in the oven and be planning a lavish summer wedding!"

Angela slapped her hand away. "You're worse than Remy!" she said, shaking her head in disbelief. "She demanded to be my maid of honor *and* begged for Nicco Morretti's address and cell-phone number all in the same text!"

The women cracked up.

"Would you hurry up and open the door? I'm roasting out here," Angela complained.

Farrah rummaged around in her oversize gold purse. "Sorry, girl, I can't find the keys. I know they're in here somewhere but…"

Loud music pierced the morning air. Fully expecting to see a group of teens cruising down the block in a lowrider, Angela glanced over her shoulder. She watched dumbfounded as a sleek, black Lamborghini turned into the food-bank parking lot.

Her eyes widened. Feeling her knees give way, she grabbed the railing to keep from falling headfirst into the bushes. *No way! It can't be!*

Angela inspected the posh sports car. It had tinted windows, diamond-studded rims, and when it rolled to a stop, the engine released an audible purr.

"Someone got lost in the wrong part of town," Farrah quipped, pulling her keys out of her purse. "Nice wheels, though, huh? Wonder how much drugs he had to sell to afford it."

Before Angela could answer, the driver's-side door lifted in the air, and Demetri slid out. Farrah gasped, dropping her keys to the ground as a hand flew to her open mouth.

"Oh, my God!"

Angela shared the same thought. Shock filled her. Not because she was surprised to see Demetri strolling through the parking lot, but because of how ridiculously handsome he looked. *It should be illegal for a man to be that fine,* she thought, admiring his casual street style. He had the confidence of a runway model and the requisite body to match. She only hoped Demetri didn't try to kiss her again, because resisting him required superhuman control, and whenever he was around she became helplessly weak.

Angela ran her eyes down the length of his body. Clad in his trademark Chicago Royals baseball cap and sunglasses, he strode through the parking lot carrying a box of doughnuts in one hand and a tray of coffee in the other. His light, refreshing cologne carried on the breeze, and his boyish grin was dreamy.

"Good morning, ladies."

Desire burned inside Angela, but she gathered herself and returned his warm greeting. "Hey, Demetri. What's up? I wasn't expecting to see you this morning."

"Why not? I told you I'd be here, and here I am."

His grin was wide and disarming. It was meant to charm, to remind her of the special moments they'd shared at Dolce Vita. And it did.

"We should get inside. There's a lot to get done today, right, Farrah?"

Her friend didn't speak. She just stood there, staring wide-eyed at Demetri.

Angela scooped the keys up off the ground and pushed them into Farrah's hands. But she didn't move. To rouse her friend from her trance, she poked her in the side with her elbow. "Come on, Farrah. Time to go inside."

"Huh?" Farrah blinked, then gave Demetri a puzzled look. "I don't mean to be rude, Mr. Morretti, but what are you doing here?"

"Call me Demetri," he said smoothly. "Angela invited me. She said you were short on volunteers, and since I had nothing to do today, I figured I'd come down and help out."

"You're here to volunteer?"

"If that's okay with you."

"Yes, yes, of course."

Demetri raised the coffee tray in the air. "I brought breakfast. If there isn't enough for everyone, I can zip back over to Dunkin' Donuts and grab some more."

"We're the only ones here so far, so that's more than enough." Farrah unlocked the door and disabled the alarm. "Welcome to the Cook County Food Bank. Please, come in."

Demetri climbed the steps and strode down the sun-filled hall behind them.

"Demetri Morretti didn't come down here to volunteer," Farrah whispered, clutching her friend's forearm. "He came here to see you!"

"I don't care." Angela unzipped her jacket. "I told you. I'm not interested in him."

"For real? You're not just saying that."

"All I care about is Demetri doing my show."

Farrah licked her glossy lips. "Good—then can I have him?"

"I don't care what anyone says," announced a tall, full-figured woman, slamming a can of kidney beans on the table. "*The Song* is rigged! And so was the last presidential election!"

Demetri chuckled. Over the past hour, he'd sorted and shelved nonperishable food items and listened in fascination to the spirited discussion the other volunteers were having. The only person who didn't join in the conversation was Angela. But Demetri suspected it was because she was too busy packing backpacks and not because she was being antisocial. He had never, in all his life, seen someone work as hard as her. She checked and double-checked the names on her list, ensured every backpack had the same number of school supplies and had taken the time to write each child a handwritten note.

"Son, you're moving too slow. You've gotta keep up."

Demetri tore his gaze away from Angela and addressed the slim, gangly man with an unkempt beard. The supervisor either didn't know who he was or didn't care. Both suited Demetri fine.

"Sorry, sir, but I'm going as fast as I can." To prove it, he scooped up the cans in his cardboard box, dropped them on the shelf and lined them up in a straight, neat line. He felt a twinge in his shoulder but smiled through his pain. "How does that look?"

"Fine, but at the rate you're going, we'll be here all day. You've only unloaded three crates in the last two hours, but Mr. Sullivan, who's thirty years your senior, has done eight!"

"Really? Wow! Good for him." Demetri chuckled, but when the supervisor crossed his fleshy arms, he halted his laughter. The man looked as if he was about to blow, and since Demetri didn't want to get tossed out of the Cook County Food Bank, he quickly unloaded the rest of the items in his crate. He was here to give back to the community *and* spend quality time with Angela, and he couldn't afford to piss anyone off—especially the ill-tempered supervisor. "I'll work harder from now on, sir. I promise."

"If you don't pick up the pace we'll be here all day, and I have plans with my old lady tonight," he said, hoisting a sack of potatoes onto the top shelf and dusting the dirt off his wide, fleshy hands. "What did you say your name was again?"

"Just call me D."

"D., you should go help Angela and the ladies and leave the sorting to us."

Demetri gestured to the black flatbed truck parked in front of the storage-room door. "There's still a lot of groceries to unload, and I'd hate to leave you hanging, sir."

"Go. I insist." The matter decided, the supervisor rested a hand on Demetri's shoulder and steered him across the storage room. "Angela, this fine young man is going to help you and your team for the rest of the morning."

Angela kept her eyes on the ribbon she was tying into a large, elaborate bow.

"Angela's a little intense," the man said, lowering his voice. "But she's the best volunteer here. Don't worry, son. You're in good hands."

Demetri didn't doubt it. Angela did it all and made it look easy. He'd been watching her on the sly for hours and marveled at her humility in serving others. Her physical beauty was striking, but he was attracted to her mind more than anything.

Sunlight poured through the window and cast a bright glow around Angela. Dressed in a belted blouse and tights, her hair cascading down her shoulders, she looked like a beautiful brown angel. And she was. After seeing her cheerfully answer the phones, pack dozens of food hampers for single mothers and clean the freezer from top to bottom, he realized Angela Kelly was an unstoppable one-woman show.

And he wanted her more than he'd ever wanted anyone.

Where the hell is Nichola? he wondered, stealing another glance at his watch. He'd called her hours ago, and she'd promised to be at the center by noon. It was twelve-thirty, and he still hadn't seen any sign of her.

Taking his cell phone out of his pocket, he checked for missed calls or texts. He had dozens of texts but none from Nichola. He considered calling her again, but when he spotted the elderly woman in the peach blouse giving him the evil eye, he shoved his cell phone back into his pocket. "What needs to be done?" he asked.

"Nothing. I got this. Just relax."

"Angela, I'm here to help, so let me."

Her eyebrows were furrowed, and she looked worried. "Englewood Elementary School was severely damaged during the thunderstorm we had a few weeks back, and the students were left with practically nothing. This project is near and dear to my heart and I want the backpacks to be perfect."

"I know, and don't worry. I'm not going to screw anything up," he said, rolling up his shirtsleeves. "Just tell me what you want me to do, and I'll do it."

Angela gestured to the wooden table to her left. "Put a box of crayons, a ruler and a spiral notebook in each backpack." She wore a sheepish smile, one that caused her eyes to sparkle like diamonds. "Thanks, Demetri. As usual, I've fallen way behind, and Mr. Crews is mad at me."

"I bet. That brother doesn't play," Demetri said, wearing a wry smile. "He should enlist in the U.S. Army. He'd make one hell of a drill sergeant!"

They shared a laugh. As they worked, they talked about the weather, movies they were anxious to see and the Fourth of July extravaganza his foundation was throwing.

"Angela, I'd love if you and your friends could come," Demetri said, glancing at her. "The event is for a great cause, and all the money raised will go toward sending disadvantaged kids to private school and junior college."

"When is it, and where is it being held?"

He thought hard but drew a blank. "I can't remember."

"Are you actually involved in the organization or just the face?"

"Just because I don't run to the papers or post it on Facebook every time I make a charitable donation doesn't mean I don't give."

"Million-dollar checks are wonderful, Demetri, but the greatest thing you can give a kid is the gift of time. They'll probably never remember what toy they got from your foundation, but they'll never forget the time they spent with their hero."

"I never asked to be a role model."

"Well, you are, and it's time you started acting like it."

Demetri folded his arms. "What's that supposed to mean?"

"Whether you like it or not, you're the face of the Chicago Royals franchise and idolized by practically every kid in this city," she explained, hurling a box of crayons into a pink Hello Kitty backpack. "Quit bellyaching about how it sucks to be famous and use your stardom for good. Read to schoolchildren, play ball in the park with neighborhood kids and, for goodness' sake, get to know the families who use the services offered by your foundation."

Demetri stood there, stunned by her criticism and the harshness of her tone. He felt small, and guilt troubled his conscience. It wasn't every day he got put in his place, and Angela's words stung. "I'm not a bad guy."

"I never said you were," she countered, "but the next time you're tempted to complain about the media hounding you or have a pity party in your twenty-room lakefront mansion, remember all the Chicago kids who look up to you."

Silence fell between them. For the next hour, Demetri worked side by side with Angela but didn't say a word. Not because he was mad, but because the tension in the room was high, and he didn't know what to say to break the silence. Her words stuck with him, played over and over again in his mind. Was Angela right? Was he a spoiled, rich athlete who did nothing but complain? Had he allowed the trappings of success and fame to make him bitter?

"Lunch is ready!" Farrah announced, sticking her head inside the storage room and waving her hands wildly in the air. "Y'all get in here and eat before my gumbo gets cold!"

A cheer erupted from the group, and everyone sped out the door.

"Aren't you going to eat?"

"I will, after I finish the rest of the backpacks." Angela stood and walked up the aisle. Slowly and carefully, she searched the shelf for more boxes of cartoon character–themed fruit snacks. "Go ahead and eat, Demetri. I bet you're starving. You've been working hard all morning."

"Not as hard as you."

Angela's shoulders tensed when Demetri moved to stand directly behind her. He was so close that she could hear him breathing.

Turning around, she pressed her back flat against the shelf. Her eyes settled on his lips. Desire swept over her, mercilessly battering her inflamed body. Angela had to find a way to withstand the heat in order to overcome the power he held over her.

Conversation and laughter flowed out of the kitchen, reminding Angela that they weren't alone, that one of the other volunteers could walk in at any minute.

"We need to talk."

"We're talking now."

"Are you mad at me?"

His words floored her. "No. Why would I be mad at you?"

"Because I've been a terrible role model for Chicago kids."

Angela wore an apologetic smile. "You came down here to volunteer, not to listen to me gripe. I'm sorry. It won't happen again."

Demetri touched a hand to her waist, and her heart stood still.

"Don't censor yourself around me. I find your honesty refreshing."

"Then why did you barge into my studio two weeks ago and threaten to sue me?"

"To get your attention," he said smoothly.

Angela wasn't buying it but didn't argue the point. To keep from staring at Demetri, she fixed her eyes on the storage-room door, watching to make sure no one was coming.

"We need to finalize the details of the interview, and the sooner the better."

"Yeah, right, the interview," she said, tearing her gaze away from the door. "Why don't you come by the station one day next week?"

"You had me banned from the building, remember? And besides, I'd prefer something less formal and more relaxed."

"Um, okay. What did you have in mind?"

Demetri moved closer, lowered his voice. "Dinner, at my place, tomorrow night."

"I already have plans."

"Break them."

"I can't," Angela said, shaking her head. "My dad has been looking forward to the Harlem Globetrotters show for weeks, and I promised I'd meet him and my brother."

"I'd hate to piss off Pops." He gave a hearty chuckle. "All right, let's do lunch instead."

"I'll have to check to see if my producer's available," she explained. "Salem normally doesn't work weekends, but I have a feeling she'll make an exception for you."

"Mrs. Velasquez is not invited. It's an intimate lunch for two."

Playing with her necklace gave Angela something to do with her hands. Something that wouldn't get her in trouble. But when Demetri stepped forward, she braced her hands against his chest, which was what she'd been itching to do from the moment he'd barged into her studio.

"I'm going to make you an authentic Italian meal and you're going to love it."

"No," she corrected, "your personal chef is going to cook, and you're going to pass the food off as your own!"

Demetri shook his head. "I don't need to. My dad taught me and my brothers how to cook at a very young age, and I can really throw down in the kitchen."

I bet you can throw down in the bedroom, too.

"I can't stop thinking about that kiss."

"Really? I forgot all about it."

A grin broke out across his face. "Is that right?"

"Yeah, it was terrible. The worst I've ever had."

"Then I'll have to redeem myself."

A warm sensation fell over Angela when Demetri crushed her lips with his mouth. Angela had no control over what happened next. At least that was what she told herself as their hands stroked and caressed and fondled each other.

Lust consumed her. Fully. His kiss was magic, and his touch shot a thousand bolts of electricity up her spine. Overwhelmed with desire, and the adrenaline coursing through her veins, Angela boldly kissed him back. But she didn't stop there. She pushed a hand under his shirt and stroked the length of his chest. His pecs were firm, his biceps were smooth to the touch, and his rock-hard abs were as perfect as she had imagined.

Caressing his powerful upper body turned Angela on. They stood there, in the middle of the aisle, pawing each other. Her body trembled, hard and fast, as his lips, tongue and hands aroused her.

Angela closed her eyes, savoring the moment. She couldn't believe it. She was standing in the food-bank storage room, kissing Demetri Morretti. It was their second kiss in two days, but this one was more passionate, more urgent and so damn erotic her panties were drenched with desire. When Demetri slid his tongue into her mouth and teased her own, she released a loud, savage moan.

"Demetri, where are you? It's showtime!"

Angela jumped back. Her heart was beating in double time, and her thoughts were a scattered mess. Her eyes scanned the room, searching for the owner of the shrill, high-pitched voice. Demetri's publicist pranced up the aisle with a cameraman and fashionably dressed entourage in tow. They were holding gigantic shopping bags and frantically snapping pictures with their cell phones.

Resting a hand on her chest, Angela took a moment to compose herself. Her heart was beating so fast, so out of control, she feared she was having a heart attack.

"Smile," Nichola shouted, clapping her hands. "This is being broadcasted live!"

Then a thin, blond man pointed a camera at them, and for the second time in twenty-four hours, Angela was sure she was going to die of embarrassment.

Chapter 11

"Get that camera out of her face." Demetri slid into the cameraman's line of vision and covered the camera lens with his hands. "Shut it off now."

"Sorry, Mr. Morretti. I didn't mean any harm. I was just doing my job."

The guy lowered the camera to his side, and Angela sighed in relief. Glancing down at her clothes, she ensured nothing was unbuttoned or unzipped and adjusted her ivory blouse.

"Demetri, relax." Nichola dumped her shopping bags on the nearest table and rushed over, all smiles and giggles. "This is Jay, your new personal videographer."

"My new what?" Gritting his teeth, he threw his hands out at his side and glanced around the room. "Nichola, what is all of this?"

"What? You told me to buy school supplies and bring them to the Cook County Food Bank, so here I am. Just like you asked."

"Yeah, but I never told you to bring a cameraman and a huge entourage."

"I know. That was my brilliant idea," she said proudly. "We've already filmed the fans and interviewed the food bank director, Mr. Crews. He's quite the character, huh?"

"Fans? What fans?"

Nichola strode over to the window and gestured outside. "Those fans," she said, pointing at the crowd gathered in the parking lot and spilling out onto the side streets. "Don't worry. I brought your security guys in to keep an eye on your Lamborghini. If anyone gets too close, they'll bring them down with ease."

Angela watched Demetri shuffle over to the window. He looked like a man who had the weight of the world on his shoulders. She actually felt sorry for him and wished she could do something to help. He'd come down to the food bank to volunteer, but all his publicist cared about was turning his good deed into a sensational news story.

"Why are there so many people here? I didn't tell anyone I'd be at the food bank."

"That was me again," Nichola said, giggling. "When you called, I posted the info on all the social-media sites, and your fans came out to show their support. Isn't that wonderful?"

"No, Nichola, it's not."

"Of course it is! Think about all the great press you're going to get and how you being here will draw attention to the needs of the food bank."

Curious about what items Demetri's publicist had bought, Angela moved over to the table and peeked inside the shopping bags. There were thousands of dollars' worth of school supplies, and when Angela saw the netbook computers and electronic dictionaries, she let out a shriek.

"This is awesome! Now we have enough school supplies to make backpacks for every student at Englewood Elementary!"

"Angela, are you sure? I'd hate for you to run out of supplies again."

"I'm positive. Thanks so much, Demetri. This is very kind of you."

He shook his head. "Don't thank me. I didn't do the shopping. I just footed the bill!"

"I don't think we've met. I'm Nichola Caruso, Demetri's publicist and personal assistant." Draping her long, thin arms through Demetri's, she leaned casually against his shoulder. "I keep this guy in line, and I love every second of it!"

"I'm Angela Kelly. It's a pleasure to meet you."

"Nichola is a huge fan of your show," Demetri said. "She watches it every day."

"Not every day. Just when there's nothing else on." Her smile was thin, as fake as her spray tan, and when she squeezed Demetri's forearm, her breasts jiggled under her low-cut designer top. "We better get going. I don't want us to be late."

"Late for what? I don't have anything planned today."

"We're visiting sick kids at the children's hospital this afternoon," she explained. "They're expecting us at one o'clock sharp."

Demetri released a deep breath. "Okay, I'll go, but the camera guy isn't coming."

"Of course he is! Why do you think I hired him?"

"No cameras, Nichola."

"Why not?"

"Because this visit to the children's hospital isn't about me. It's about those courageous kids and their families. Pay the videographer and send him home."

"Okay, okay, he won't film you at the hospital," she agreed. "But I'm not sending him home. Jay's flying with us to L.A."

"What's in L.A.?"

"You're making three nightclub appearances tonight, and in the morning you're shooting a Got Milk? commercial."

Demetri stared at Angela, and a smile fell across his lips. "Cancel it. I have plans tomorrow afternoon. Plans I'm not breaking."

"But, Demetri—"

"Nichola, this is not open for discussion. Reschedule it for another day or cancel it altogether. I don't care either way."

"Fine. You're the boss," she said with a shrug. "We'll be waiting outside."

The group shuffled out of the room, wearing long faces, and the storage-room door closed with a bang. When the room was clear, Demetri faced her. "Angela, I'm sorry. I asked

Nichola to drop off some school supplies, but I had no idea she'd bring a cameraman and ten of her closest girlfriends to use as human props."

"Demetri, you don't need to apologize. And thanks again for all of the stuff."

"I could come back when I finish at the hospital and help you finish the backpacks."

"I'll be fine. If I need help, I'll just ask one of the other volunteers."

"No, you won't!"

Angela laughed. "So, I like things to be perfect. Sue me!"

"You have to learn to relax and live in the moment." He drew a hand down her cheek. "I love when the unexpected happens. Don't you?"

"Yeah, as long as it isn't taped and posted on YouTube!"

More laughter filled the room.

"I'm looking forward to our lunch date tomorrow."

"I'll be there at twelve o'clock sharp."

"Of course you will." A grin pinched his lips. "You're always on time, you always play by the rules, and you do everything just right. I'm hoping your good qualities will rub off on me, because according to the media, I'm a screwup who does everything wrong."

His words gave Angela pause. There was something in his tone that troubled her, that made her feel guilty. Her gaze moved over his face. He didn't look like the terse, surly athlete who'd stormed her studio weeks earlier. Instead he appeared sensitive and vulnerable, and there was nothing cocky about that.

"I'll call you later to give you my address."

"But you don't have my phone number."

"Yeah, I do. I've had it for weeks. Got it from your station manager."

"Then why did you ask me for my number last night at Dolce Vita?"

"Because I wanted to see if you were feeling me." He grinned. "I'm glad you are."

He bent down, kissed her on both cheeks and then turned and strode out of the storage room.

Angela sashayed through Woodfield Mall with a smile on her lips and glitzy shopping bags in her hands. Slipping on her diamond-studded sunglasses, she sailed through the sliding glass doors and out into the warm spring night.

The air smelled of tobacco, but despite the putrid odor, her stomach released a loud, audible growl. Angela had been so busy trying on clothes and fretting over how she looked in each outfit, she'd forgotten to eat lunch. But after countless trips between the clearance racks and the fitting room in her favorite store, she'd finally found an outfit to wear for her lunch date tomorrow with Demetri. And not just any old thing. A dress that would make the man drool all over his Chicago Royals jersey.

Angela shook her head, and the thought, out of her mind. "It's not a date. It's a business lunch," she told herself, unlocking the trunk of her car and dumping her purchases inside.

Anxious to get home and pair her dress with the right shoes and accessories, she slid into the front seat of her car and started the engine. Hearing her cell phone ring, she rummaged around in her purse until she found it.

"Hello?" she said, putting her cell phone to her ear seconds later.

"Angela, it's Salem. Sorry I didn't get back to you last night. That lousy hockey game went into triple overtime, and my husband wouldn't leave!"

Angela laughed. "It's no problem. I understand."

"How did everything go at Dolce Vita?"

You don't want to know, she thought, releasing a deep sigh. But instead of ratting out her crew to her boss, she said, "Everything went great. We did a ton of interviews, got some

FREE Merchandise is 'in the Cards' for you!

Dear Reader,

We're giving away FREE MERCHANDISE!

Seriously, we'd like to reward you for reading this novel by giving you **FREE MERCHANDISE** worth over **$20**. And no purchase is necessary!

You see the Jack of Hearts sticker above? Paste that sticker in the box on the Free Merchandise Voucher inside. Return the Voucher promptly...and we'll send you valuable Free Merchandise!

Thanks again for reading one of our novels—and enjoy your Free Merchandise with our compliments!

Pam Powers

Pam Powers

P.S. Look inside to see what Free Merchandise is **"in the cards"** for you!

We'd like to send you two free books like the one you are enjoying now. Your two books have a combined price of over $10, but they are yours to keep absolutely FREE! We'll even send you 2 wonderful surprise gifts. You can't lose!

REMEMBER: Your Free Merchandise, consisting of **2 Free Books** and **2 Free Gifts**, is worth over $20.00! No purchase is necessary, so please send for your Free Merchandise today.

FREE MERCHANDISE VOUCHER

2 FREE
BOOKS
and
2 FREE
GIFTS

Please send my Free Merchandise, consisting of
2 Free Books and **2 Free Mystery Gifts**.
I understand that I am under no obligation to buy
anything, as explained on the back of this card.

168/368 XDL GELZ

Please Print

FIRST NAME

LAST NAME

ADDRESS

APT.# CITY

STATE/PROV. ZIP/POSTAL CODE

NO PURCHASE NECESSARY!

K-714-FM13

amazing shots from the roof and taped a group of college kids singing the show's theme song!"

"Everything went okay? Really? That's not what Phil and the guys said."

"What?" The word blasted out of Angela's mouth. "What exactly did they say?"

"They said you went to the ladies' room and never came back!"

"No. They. Didn't." Angela was gripping her BlackBerry phone so hard, she was surprised it didn't shatter into a million pieces. "They're lying! That's not what happened!"

"Okay," she said slowly, "so why don't you tell me what really happened, because Phil's version of events was just too fanciful to believe."

Slumping back in her seat, Angela recounted every moment of the previous night—except for the kiss she'd shared with Demetri and the time they'd spent alone together in the VIP lounge. Thoughts of Demetri kept Angela from firing up her car, driving to the station and kicking Phil's country ass. How dare he double-cross her! Was he in cahoots with the lead anchor or just trying to make himself look good? "Wait until I see Phil on Monday," she thought aloud. "I'm going to make him wish we'd never met!"

"Slow your roll!" Salem laughed. "Leave Phil and the rest of his crew to me. I have something extra-special in store for them."

A sigh of relief escaped Angela's lips. "I'd never bail on an assignment," she said, shivering at the thought. "I'm so glad you believe me, Salem. It means the world to me."

"Of course I believe you! You're one of the most diligent and hardworking newscasters I've ever met."

Angela smiled, but inside she was still fighting mad.

"I've got good news and bad news. Which do you want first?"

"The bad. I'll forget all about it when I hear the good news."

"I presented your proposal this morning at the producers' meeting, and the team hated it. They said the topic was too dark and heavy for *Eye on Chicago.*"

Angela's shoulders sagged in defeat. To ward off tears, she pressed her eyes shut and bit the inside of her cheek. She felt as if she'd been kicked in the stomach. The pain in her chest was so sharp, she could barely breathe.

"They want to keep the show fun and current," Salem explained, her tone loud and exuberant. "We want you to play it up for the cameras and flirt even more with your male celebrity guests. That's your niche, Angela! That's where you shine!"

Strangling a groan, Angela slumped back in her seat, feeling deflated and defeated. She was more than just a pretty face, and she had the education to prove it. Working for WJN-TV was a dream come true, but Angela was sick of having the same argument with her boss. Viewers tuned in to see her on Thursday nights—not the show's producers—so why was she letting *them* tell *her* what to do?

"What's the good news?" she asked, unable to hide her disappointment and anxious to get off the phone.

"Earl is having hip surgery next month, and he'll be out six to eight weeks."

"That's too bad. I hope everything goes okay."

"How do you feel about filling in for him?"

Angela shot up in her seat. "Seriously? You want me to do the live morning show?"

"Yeah, I think you'd be great," she said with a laugh. "I already know you'll be on time. You're always the first one at the station!"

"Howard will never go for it. He hates having female co-hosts."

"Don't worry. We go way back. I can handle him."

"Do you think the head-ups will go for it?"

"They already have!"

Angela squealed like a teenage girl on a roller coaster. "Really? No way!"

"Once they heard that you'd scored an exclusive sit-down interview with Demetri Morretti at his Lake County estate, they were putty in my hands."

"But…Demetri hasn't agreed to be on my show."

"Not yet," Salem quipped, "but he will. I have complete faith in you."

"I'm glad one of us does." Angela felt her smile fade and her excitement wane. Resisting the urge to scream in frustration, she took a deep breath and channeled positive thoughts. None came. All she could think about was how her good mood had been shot to hell. First, her crew lied about her and then her boss fabricated a story about her show to impress the studio heads. What else could possibly go wrong today?

"Stay close to your phone, Angela. I might need you to cover the hot-dog-eating contest out at Six Flags this afternoon."

It's true, she decided, shaking her head. *Bad things do happen in threes!*

"I have to run. The in-laws are coming over for dinner, and I'm still in my bathrobe."

"Okay. Talk to you later."

"Oh, and, Angela, one more thing." Her tone grew serious. "The next time Demetri Morretti shows up at the food bank, text me immediately, because *that's* breaking news!"

Chapter 12

"Are you sure you don't want me to stay?" Nichola asked, climbing down the front steps of Demetri's Lake County estate and joining him in his Mediterranean-style garden. "Angela Kelly's a piranha in Gucci pumps. You might need backup."

"Go home, Nichola. I'll be fine." Demetri pointed his silver watering can at the terra-cotta pots and moved slowly down the row of leafy plants. He wanted his publicist to leave so he could go inside and get ready for his date in peace. It had been months since he'd invited a woman to his house, and he wanted everything to be perfect—the food, the ambience, his appearance. Angela was in a league of her own, and Demetri knew if he wanted to make headway with her this afternoon he had to bring his A game. "Have fun at your sister's bachelorette party."

"I have a bad feeling about Angela Kelly coming here."

"Don't worry. It's all good. We made a truce."

Nichola's eyes thinned and shrunk into a glare. "You're not interested in her romantically, are you?"

"Who, me?" Demetri coughed to clear the lump in his throat. He didn't want anyone—especially his brothers—to know he was interested in Angela. In part because he knew they'd laugh him out of the room. He was attracted to the very woman who had dissed him on national television, and more shocking, he'd been thinking about her nonstop since they'd kissed at Dolce Vita. *If that isn't crazy, I don't know what is!* he thought, shaking his head.

"This is a business lunch," he said. "We'll talk, and then she'll be on her way."

"And you're sure you don't want me to stay and run interference?"

"I'm a grown man. I don't need anyone to hold my hand or fight my battles," he said, trying to keep the lid on his frustration. "And besides, Angela Kelly isn't a threat. I can handle her."

"Speak of the devil..."

Demetri glanced over his shoulder. When he saw Angela exit her navy blue jeep, the fine hairs on the back of his neck shot up. Wide-eyed, he watched her glide up the mosaic-tile steps with the grace of the First Lady. Her walk was poetry in motion. Mesmerized, he stood beside the decorative oak bench, speechless. Angela's belted mustard dress showcased her curves, and her ankle-tie pumps gave her a sexy bad-girl edge. Her classy, sophisticated look was a home run, and he was so aroused by the sight of her mouthwatering shape, his brain turned to mush.

Smiling brightly, Angela waved as she approached. Her long, black hair flapped wildly in the light spring breeze, drawing his gaze up from her hips to her beautiful oval face.

Demetri felt the urge to run, to sprint full speed ahead toward her. It was impossible to be around Angela and not feel good. Yesterday at the food bank, they'd talked and joked and laughed with ease. He'd felt like his old, jovial self, like the person he used to be before the media started gunning for him and his injuries began piling up.

"Welcome to my home." Taking her hand, Demetri leaned in and kissed Angela on each cheek. It was a standard Italian greeting, but there was nothing innocent about the surge of blood flow he felt below his belt. He wanted to take Angela in his arms and tease her soft, moist lips with his mouth, but for now holding her hand was enough. "You're early. I wasn't expecting you for another half an hour."

"It's raining in the city, and the streets are crazy, so I decided to leave early," she explained. "Surprisingly, I made it here in record time."

Nichola appeared, like a puff of smoke, scowling in earnest. She looked Angela up and down but addressed Demetri. "I'll see you tomorrow," she said, her voice terse. "Don't forget, the rep from Rolex International will be here at one to discuss your new signature line."

"I won't forget. Have a good time with your girls tonight."

"I will, but if you need anything, just call. It doesn't matter how late." She gave a curt nod and then hustled down the steps to her white sports car.

Angela was glad to see Demetri's publicist go. Not because she wanted to be alone with him, but because there was something about the petite strawberry blonde that unnerved her.

"Perfect timing," Demetri said, squeezing her hand. "I was just finishing up in the garden."

"You garden?"

"I love it. Being outside and working with my hands is very therapeutic. If not for the helicopters buzzing around here all day, I'd probably sleep on the lawn!"

"A baseball star with a green thumb? Who would have thought?"

Demetri chuckled. "I'm no Martha Stewart, but I'm getting there."

The estate was as calm as it was scenic and dotted with dozens of trees, flower beds and white stone structures. The soothing sound of rushing water added to the tranquillity of Demetri's ten-thousand-square-foot home. The fragrant scent of jasmine was heavy in the air.

"Wow, your garden has everything. Fruits, herbs, vegetables, even colored tulips…" Angela broke off speaking and pointed at the gazebo. "The flowers you sent me at Dolce Vita came from your garden?"

"Yeah, I handpicked them." His smile was proud. "I read on your blog how much you love tulips, so I figured I'd make you an original Demetri Morretti bouquet."

His words stunned her. There was more to him than bar brawls and drag racing. "What were you doing poking around on my blog?" she asked, her tone playful. "You weren't trying to hack into it, were you?"

"No, I was doing some research." He winked and gave her hand a light squeeze. "Do you mind waiting inside the living room while I run upstairs to change?"

"You don't need to change. You look great." Angela immediately wished she could stick the words back in her mouth. But it was true. He looked handsome in his white, cuffed shirt and khaki shorts, and when a wide, boyish grin broke out across his lips, Angela knew she'd said too much.

"I'm glad we didn't meet up at a restaurant or bar," he said, still smiling. "Because I'd have to beat the guys off of you with my lucky baseball bat!"

Angela's mouth dried. His words floored her, and when he gave her another peck on the cheek, goose bumps erupted over her skin. It was bad enough Demetri was still holding her hand, but now she had to contend with the tingles pricking her flesh, too.

"Let's eat. Everything's set up on the patio for us."

"Lunch can wait," Angela said. "First, you have to give me a tour of this stunning estate."

Demetri chuckled. "It would be my pleasure. Just let me buzz one of the groundsmen and ask them to bring up a golf cart."

"Can we walk instead?"

"Are you sure? It's almost two acres."

"I'm sure. It's gorgeous out here, and since I skipped my

morning session with my trainer, I could really use the exercise."

Angela heard her cell phone ring but ignored it. Rodney had been blowing up her phone all day, but she didn't feel like talking to him. Or seeing him, either. Her dad had invited him to the Harlem Globetrotters show, and Angela would rather skip the game than listen to her brother's tired apologies. "How long have you lived here?"

"Seven years. I have a condo near the Royals training facility, but I spend most of my time here. It's peaceful out here and I love being near the lake..."

As they strode around the grounds, discussing all of the unique features of his lavish, custom-made home, Angela felt herself start to relax. Flirting and laughing with Demetri was exhilarating, and she loved his fun, playful mood. It was hard to believe this was the same guy who'd stormed into her studio weeks ago and threatened to sue her. But it was. And although Angela was anxious to finalize the details of their interview, she sensed that now was not the right time and decided she would broach the subject during lunch.

"I saw your report from Club Eclipse last night," Demetri said, leading her past the greenhouse. "Every time I turn to WJN-TV, you're on it. Do you work twenty-four seven?"

"No. I have days off just like everybody else."

He raised an eyebrow and wore a teasing smile. "And what do you do on these supposed days off?"

"I go to the movies, peruse used-book stores and go club hopping with my girls. You know, the usual single-girl stuff!"

Demetri chuckled. "So, you're not seeing anyone special right now?"

"No one worth mentioning."

"You like kicking it with athletes."

"No," she corrected, "I like sports. There's a big difference."

He wore a confused face. "Care to elaborate?"

"I'm a tomboy in a skirt, and guys love that I don't mind getting down and dirty."

Angela laughed when Demetri's jaw fell open.

"I grew up playing sports, fishing and going to auto shows with my dad and younger brother, so naturally I get along really well with guys," she said with a shrug.

"Your mom didn't mind you playing with G.I. Joe instead of Barbie?" he teased.

"She was never around, and when she died five years ago, I grew even closer to my dad." Angela didn't want to talk about her mom or the pain of never really knowing her, so she moved the conversation along. "I enjoy activities the average woman doesn't, and men like that." She paused. "And for the record, I don't pursue men. They pursue me."

"But you've dated an athlete in every major sport."

"No, that's not true. I've never dated a hockey player or a soccer star." Angela wore a cheeky smile. "But I'm still young. There's plenty of time for that."

"Not if things go the way I hope." Desire twinkled in his eyes and warmed his rich, smooth baritone. Demetri slid a hand around her waist and hugged her to his side. "You must be starving. How about some lunch?"

When they reached the sprawling multilevel patio, which was handsomely furnished with tan couches, circular tables and a stone fireplace, Demetri pulled out her chair. Once she was seated, he filled her glass with Chianti and her gold-rimmed plate with lobster and pasta.

"This is some house," Angela said, admiring her lavish surroundings. The estate was unlike anything she had ever seen. She was blown away by the sheer size and grandeur of the twenty-room mansion. "Do you live here alone?"

"Not if I can help it!" Demetri chuckled. "My younger cousins crash here a few nights a week, and my parents and brothers stay with me whenever they're in town."

"Wow, that's different."

"That's the Italian way. My family means everything to me, and without them I'm nothing." He paused to taste his wine. "My happiest memories are with my relatives, and even though they can be a pain in the ass sometimes, I love when we all get together and hang out."

"Is that why you're taking eighty-five family members with you on vacation?"

Demetri nodded. "I've been planning these trips since my rookie season, and each trip is better than the last. We're going on a Caribbean cruise in August, and I'm real hyped about it."

"I love my dad, but I couldn't imagine traveling with him for a week, let alone a month!"

"Then you should consider joining us. All of your travel expenses will be covered, and for three weeks you won't have to worry about a thing."

"Demetri, that's crazy." Angela draped a silk napkin onto her lap and picked up her gold utensils. "I can't go with you and your family overseas. They probably hate me for trashing you on my show, and besides, we barely know each other."

"I know a lot about you."

"Sure you do," she teased. "You've been secretly stalking me for weeks. I knew it!"

A knowing smile crossed his lips. Lowering his fork, he studied her closely. "You graduated from the University of Chicago with a degree in communications, you hate musicals, you're addicted to coffee and designer shoes, and the only movie to ever make you cry is a French film called *A Kiss in Paris*. And not because you thought it was a great love story, but because the acting was so bad!"

Angela groaned and covered her face with her hands. "You read the first entry in my blog? The one way back in 2004?"

"No," he said, correcting her. "I read *every* entry."

"Now I'm really embarrassed. That means you saw all my

pictures in my video diary. I had terrible hair when I was in college and no fashion sense whatsoever."

"No, you didn't, and you looked great in your volleyball uniform." Demetri winked and pointed his fork at his chest. "I made your Hot 100 List that year, so you know I'm happy!"

"I typed that blog while I was watching your rookie game, and every time you came to bat, I got goose bumps," she confessed. "You were amazing that night, Demetri."

"My rookie season was the best year of my life."

"Was? Don't you still love playing baseball?"

"I'm getting old, and—"

Angela cut him off. "Old? You're only thirty-two!"

"Yeah, but I've been in the league since I was twenty." He chewed his lobster slowly and then took a long drink of wine. "If I just had to play ball, I could deal, but the paparazzi, the crazed fans and the constant demands on my time are taxing. I'm not complaining or bitching about how unfair life is, but sometimes the glare of the spotlight is just too bright."

Angela nodded. "I've heard other celebrities say the same thing. From the outside looking in, it seems like you have the perfect life, but I guess things aren't always as it seems."

"You can say that again." He wore a wry smile, but his voice betrayed his true feelings. "I love this estate, and it has a ton of cool stuff in it, but sometimes I feel like a caged animal. There are so many places I can't go, so many things I can't do anymore unless I take my security, and sometimes it's just not worth the hassle."

"What do you miss doing?"

"Little things, like going to the movies, surfing at Montrose Beach or taking the L line up to the field and—"

"Liar!" she shrieked. "You do *not* miss riding the smelly, crowded L train!"

"You're right. I don't. Bad example."

Laughter bubbled out of Angela's lips, and Demetri smiled.

And when he served dessert several minutes later, and she broke out in a cheer, he had a good hard chuckle.

"I love strawberry gelato," Angela cooed, spooning some into her mouth and savoring the cold, refreshing taste. "I could eat a whole tub. And I have!"

"Do you like to play pool?"

"Of course. Who doesn't?"

"Practically every woman I've ever met!" Demetri chuckled. "After we finish dessert, we should go inside and hang out in my media room. We can play pool, listen to music and…"

Hearing her cell phone ring, Angela discreetly slid a hand inside her purse and rummaged around for her BlackBerry. When she saw her brother's name pop up on the screen, she hurled her cell phone back into the bottom of her purse.

"Your phone's been ringing off the hook all afternoon." Demetri wore a pensive expression on his face. "Someone must want to reach you bad."

"Yeah, probably to ask for another loan," she grumbled, rolling her eyes to the gray, overcast sky. "I wish Rodney would quit blowing up my phone and lose my number altogether."

"Rodney? Who's that? An ex-boyfriend or something?"

"Yuck." Angela wrinkled her nose. "Rodney's my kid brother."

"And you guys don't talk?"

"Not anymore."

Demetri sat straight in his chair. "Why not?"

"I'd rather not talk about it."

"Did he put you in harm's way?"

"No, of course not. Rodney would never hurt me." Angela sucked her teeth. "Lying and stealing is right up his alley, though."

"Angela, you should try to work things out with your brother. He's your flesh and blood. Don't ever forget that. Friends come and go, but family is forever."

"I'm so mad at Rodney, I don't want anything to do with him ever again."

"Forgiveness isn't forgetting or condoning bad behavior, Angela. It's a gift to yourself."

His words gave her pause, struck a chord with her.

"For years, I was mad at the world and everyone who had ever betrayed me, but ever since I started reading the teachings of eastern philosophers, my attitude's changed for the better." Leaning forward, Demetri took her hand in his and gave it a light squeeze. His touch was gentle, not what she'd expected, but welcome.

"Forgiveness is a gift you give to yourself, because once you forgive the person who hurt you, you're free of the hurt, anger and resentment that's been eating you up inside."

Scared her emotions would get the best of her and she'd dissolve into tears, Angela looked up into the sky. A curtain of dark, thick clouds eclipsed the sun, and the air held the scent of rain. Angela didn't know when the weather had taken a turn for the worst, probably somewhere between dessert and her third glass of Chianti, but she'd been too busy chatting to notice. "What you're saying makes sense, Demetri, but it's hard to forgive someone who keeps hurting you. Rodney's twenty-one, but he still acts like a teenager," she complained. "It's time he quit running the streets and did something productive with his life instead of stealing from me."

"It sounds like he's going through a rough time. You should be there for him."

"And let him rip me off again? No way."

"Haven't you ever done something you regretted? Something you wish you could undo?" he asked softly. "I know I have. Too many times to count."

"I've made mistakes, but I've never intentionally hurt anyone."

Yeah, but if your dad knew how you paid for your uni-

versity tuition, he'd be deeply ashamed, said a small voice in her head.

Angela stared down at her dessert bowl. She didn't want to think about her freshman year in college or the job she'd reluctantly taken after her scholarship had fallen through. Those memories belonged in the past, hidden in the deepest corner of her mind. Her father would never forgive her if he knew what she'd done, and she couldn't bear to disappoint her dad. Not after all the sacrifices he'd made for her over the years. "Let's talk about something more interesting," she said, anxious to change the subject, "like you being a guest on *Eye on Chicago.*"

He lifted the wine bottle and tipped some into her glass. "I checked my schedule, and I'm free on May seventeenth. Does that work for you?"

"I'll make it work!"

Thunder boomed, and streaks of lightning lit up the sky.

"We better get inside before it starts to—" Demetri broke off speaking and jumped to his feet when raindrops pelted his face. "Follow me!"

Angela swiped her purse off the nearby chair and grabbed Demetri's outstretched hand. Moving as fast as her high-heel-clad feet would take her, she sprinted across the patio, through the French doors and into the kitchen.

Scared she was going to drip water on the white marble floor, Angela stood perfectly still on the mat in front of the back door. The main floor was as wide and as long as a football field and decked out in the best home decor money could buy. Soaring columns, dark velvet drapes and leather furniture gave the room a strong masculine feel, and the burgundy color scheme was striking.

"I'll be right back," Demetri said. "I'm going to go grab some towels."

Shaking uncontrollably, Angela rubbed her hands over her

shoulders. Her hair was a tangled mess, her dress was stuck to her wet body, and water was oozing from her high heels.

A loud crash drew her gaze to the side window. Outside, the wind battered the plants hanging on the porch. It was raining so hard, Angela couldn't even see the pool. To stop her teeth from chattering, she clamped her lips together and rocked slowly from side to side.

"Sorry I took so long." Wearing a concerned face, Demetri wrapped the fluffy, white towel he was holding around her shoulders and drew her to his side. His scent had a calming, soothing effect on her. Closing her eyes, she rested her head on his chest. His shirt was damp, but Angela felt warm, cozy and safe.

"I could stay here with you forever like this," he murmured against her ear.

Me, too, Angela thought but didn't dare say. *This feels so right. You feel so right.*

"Are you okay?"

"I'm fine. It was just a little rain."

"I'm not talking about the rain."

Angela's eyes fluttered open, and when his dark, predatory gaze slipped over her flesh, her stomach muscles tightened. Demetri was trouble. Assertive. Confident. Determined to have his way. And Angela wanted him. More than she'd ever wanted anyone before.

"You had several glasses of Chianti with lunch."

"Demetri, I'm not drunk."

"Are you sure?" he questioned, cupping her chin and cradling it in his palm. "I don't want to take any chances."

"I'm far too responsible to ever drink and drive—"

"You're not leaving."

"I'm not?" Angela gave him a puzzled, bewildered look. "Then why are you worried about how much I had to drink?"

Lowering his mouth, he brushed it ever so gently against

her lips. "Because when you wake up in the morning, I want you to remember every sinfully wicked thing that's going to happen tonight."

Chapter 13

"That's it, baby! Right there! Right there!" Angela panted, gripping Demetri's head with her hands and pulling his long, nimble tongue deeper inside her. Collapsing against the mound of silk pillow cushions, she tossed and turned, wiggled and withered beneath him. His touch was electric, made her body hot and wet all over. "Damn, baby..."

His hands traveled to her breasts, reverently cupping each one. Demetri was good with his hands. No, great, the best. He kissed her nipple slow and tender with his soft, warm mouth. Angela felt her eyes roll in the back of her head. Her breathing became labored, difficult. She tried to the best of her ability to think straight. She didn't remember how they'd gotten to the master bedroom or even which floor they were on. The past hour had been a body-tingling ride, one filled with sensuous highs, delicious French kisses and so much grunting and groaning, they sounded like wild animals.

But that was exactly how Angela felt. Wild, brazen, out of control. And it was the best feeling in the world. Demetri brought out the beast in her—the naughty, erotic side she didn't even know she had. And tonight Angela didn't care about being perfect or looking perfect. All she cared about was pleasing Demetri.

Rain smacked against the bedroom windows, and although the blinds were open, the master suite was bathed in darkness. The perfume of their desire filled the air. The scent was so powerful, Angela got drunk off its fragrance. Out of sorts, the room spinning around her, she closed her eyes and stroked Demetri's broad, muscular shoulders. He knew exactly what she wanted and gave it to her. His hands knew where to go, what to do, and every flick of his tongue was more urgent and hungrier than the last.

Angela moaned his name over and over again. She couldn't help it. Without a doubt, he was the sexiest, most skilled lover she had ever had. Lying on Demetri's custom-made bed in nothing but her jewelry should have terrified Angela, but it didn't. He'd undressed her slowly with a look of admiration in his eyes. And by the time he carried her over to his king-size bed, she was desperate to make love to him. Lust filled her. Made it impossible to think, to breathe. She wanted him to touch her, to stroke her, to feel every inch of his erection inside her.

"Demetri," she whispered, her tone a breathless pant. "Come here."

He joined her at the front of the bed and wrapped his arms around her.

"We'll cuddle later. I need you inside me. *Now.*"

"Not yet, Angela. There's no rush. We have all night...." Nuzzling his chin against the curve of her ear, he whispered, "I'm going to love you like you've never been loved before, and when you come, you're going to feel the strongest emotion you've ever felt."

Well, I'll be damned, she thought, overwhelmed by the rush his words gave her.

Longing for the taste of his lips, Angela draped her arms around his shoulders and pressed her lips hard against his mouth. Demetri reeled back against the headboard. It was a deep, passionate kiss—one that put Angela in the mood for hard, fast sex. His lips tasted like wine, his kiss was as exhilarating as his touch, and his whispered promises touched the depth of her heart. Tilting her head to the side, she swirled her tongue around his mouth. She licked and sucked the tip of his tongue as if it were coated in chocolate syrup.

Demetri placed light kisses down her cheeks and along the side of her neck. Using his lips and hands to make sweet love to her flesh, he covered every inch of her body in fervent kisses and tender caresses. Using the tip of his tongue, he licked from her nipples to her stomach to the insides of her thighs. His hands traveled the length of her waist, and the finger he slipped between her legs to stroke her clit only fanned the flames.

Demetri stroked her butt with his hands. His touch made her ache for more—more sucking, more teasing, more grinding. Angela loved the way he was making her feel and couldn't get enough of his kiss. But tonight she wanted to be in control of her pleasure. She wanted to please Demetri, wanted to erase every other woman from his mind, and Angela knew just what to do to make it happen.

She eased herself onto Demetri's lap. Stroking his shoulders, she watched in anticipation as he opened his side drawer, took out a condom and rolled it onto his long, thick erection. Angela licked her lips. This was it. The moment she'd been waiting for, the moment she'd been dreaming about for weeks.

Demetri pressed a hand to her cheek and stared deep into her eyes. "Are you sure about this, Angela? I don't want you to have any regrets."

"My only regret is waiting this long."

He brushed his nose against hers, and she let out a giggle. "Quit teasing me, Demetri. I want this, and I want you."

"I'm just making sure."

Angela couldn't tell Demetri the truth, that she'd been fantasizing about him ever since he'd stormed into her television studio. Scared of where their attraction would lead, she'd told her friends, her boss and anyone else who would listen that she wasn't interested in the baseball star. But Angela couldn't deny how his touch made her feel. She felt alive, as if she were spinning upside down on a Ferris wheel. Being with Demetri was the ultimate rush, a shot of adrenaline that blew her mind. He did it for her. Made her hot, revved her engines.

And when Demetri slid his erection inside her, shivers ripped down her back. Pleasure filled her, drenched her skin like the raindrops pelting the bedroom windows. Gripping the headboard, she rotated her hips at a pace that intensified her need. Demetri whispered soft words against her ears as he nipped at her earlobes and the side of her neck. Seemingly knowing what turned her on, he cupped her breasts, then teased and sucked each erect nipple into his open mouth.

Angela moaned and screamed in ecstasy. She was losing it, coming apart at the seams. She felt exhilarated, as if she'd been shot a hundred feet in the air. A moan escaped out of her lips. Then another. Her heart was pounding, racing, dribbling like a ball. Angela never imagined a man could be this giving, this unselfish in the bedroom. Feeling tears fill her eyes, she blinked them away and bit down on her lip. Demetri ran his lips along her arms, playfully nipping and licking her warm flesh.

Angela pushed her breasts into his face, stuck her nipples into his mouth so he could have another taste. Reverently, he kissed and stroked each breast. Throwing her head back, she moaned to the high heavens. This was euphoria. The most thrilling and erotic moment of her life. Nothing compared to making love to Demetri. Nothing. Not a five-figure raise. Not a free swag bag from the Grammys. Not even meeting her idol, Diane Sawyer, at last year's Emmy Awards.

"I knew from the moment I saw you that you were the one."

A grin pinched her lips. "Was that before or *after* you threatened to sue me?"

"I was never going to sue you. I just wanted to get your attention."

"Well, *Mr. Athlete of the Year,* you certainly did that."

"Angela, I've fallen hard for you." His voice deepened,

grew thick with feeling and emotion. "You're the only woman I want. The only woman I need."

Angela stared at Demetri. His gaze was intense, locked in on hers, and he wore a dreamy, lopsided smile.

"I knew the second I walked into your studio that I was done. I tried to fight our attraction, tried to ignore it, but the harder I tried to get you out of my mind, the more I thought about you, fantasized about you and dreamed about being inside you."

I know exactly how you feel. Angela rubbed her hand along his shoulders and chest. Everything about Demetri turned her on. His voice, his scent, his sensitivity, how he tenderly caressed and kissed her. He was different. *This* was different. Tonight was about more than just sex. Her heart was in it, her soul and her mind, too. And for as long as she lived, she'd never forget how amazing it had felt when he'd kissed her for the very first time.

"I'm a hundred percent ready to commit to you, Angela. Not for a day or a week or a month, but forever." He placed his palms against her cheeks and kissed from her eyelids to her earlobes and back again. Love showed in his eyes and covered the length of his face. "Give me the opportunity to spoil you, to love you, to cook for you…"

His words left her wide-eyed and tongue-tied. Demetri had a brusque exterior and walked around with a chip on his shoulder, but inside he was a softy. The reigning bad boy of professional baseball wasn't an arrogant jerk; he was a deeply sensitive man who wore his heart on his sleeve, and each caress and kiss made her feel like a cherished jewel.

"You are absolute perfection," he praised. "You're the sassiest, most vibrant and engaging woman I've ever met. And did I mention sexy as hell?"

"I am pretty wonderful, aren't I?"

In one swift motion, Demetri flipped Angela onto her back

and pinned her hands above her head. "Yes, baby, you are, and don't you ever forget it."

Stretched out, lying face-to-face, with their bodies meshed together, Angela felt at home in Demetri's arms. He slowly slid his erection inside her, one delicious inch at a time. Clamping her legs around his waist produced the most exquisite sensation. Quivering, shaking, trembling all over, she fought to stay in the moment and in control. As Demetri loved her, he shared his heart. He spoke about their future, about all the wonderful places he wanted to take her and activities he wanted them to do. His earnest, heartfelt confession blew her away.

"You have no idea how amazing it feels being inside you...."

Angela loved everything Demetri was doing and saying. Using her fingernails, she tenderly stroked his shoulders and the length of his back. She held him, snuggled close as he quickened his pace. Angela showered kisses on his lips, along the slope of his jaw and the front of his neck. Her heart opened and filled with unspeakable love. This wasn't just a night of carnal pleasure. It was a reawakening of her soul and her entire being. There had been a hollowness in her heart for years, but tonight, in Demetri's bed, in his arms, she felt whole. But Angela didn't tell Demetri that. She never talked about her feelings and didn't really know how to. Besides, telling him the truth would only complicate things, and their relationship was already complicated enough.

Demetri hiked her legs in the air, spread her wide open. And three deep, powerful thrusts later, his climax hit. His muscles strained; his body tensed. Angela pressed her lips together to trap a scream inside, one she was sure would shatter every window in the estate. She felt as if she were outside herself, in a different world. A world filled with passion and desire and love. Demetri was a tender, gentle lover who told her she was strong and beautiful and special. Pleasing her was his only priority, and his words aroused and excited her. Never had she felt such love, such compassion in a lover's touch, and when her orgasm struck—knocking the very breath out of her—Angela knew she'd never be the same again.

Chapter 14

Demetri stared at the silver breakfast tray, realizing he'd forgotten the fruit, and strode back over to the stainless-steel fridge. He had to hurry. Angela was still sleeping in the master bedroom, and he wanted to be back upstairs with breakfast waiting on the deck before she woke up. Sunshine splashed through the open windows, and the glass chimes, hanging on the patio, tinkled as the wind whipped through the backyard.

Demetri smiled to himself. He felt exhilarated, on top of the world. As if he'd just smashed a fastball out of Skyline Field. Angela had put it on him, and not just in the bedroom. They had a deep connection, one he'd never experienced with any other woman before. Just the thought of her made him break out into an ear-to-ear grin.

As he sliced the pineapple and arranged it on the gold-rimmed plates, he relived every moment of their evening together. The long stroll around his estate, eating and chatting outside on the patio, that explosive kiss that rocked his world. He thought about their passionate lovemaking and the long, heartfelt talk they'd had afterward.

"Relationships are too complicated," she'd said, her tone matter-of-fact. "That's why I play the field and leave having husbands and babies to my girlfriends."

"I used to think that way, but things changed when I turned thirty. I started wanting a wife and a family of my own."

"My ultimate goal is to become an international news correspondent, not to have more kids than Octomom," she said with a laugh. "And I'm my working my butt off to make it happen."

"News correspondents get the toughest, most dangerous assignments," he'd pointed out, tightening his hold around her waist. Without makeup and designer clothes on, Angela looked like a fresh-faced college student, and Demetri loved how it felt having her in his arms. "They travel all over the world and are away from their friends and family for long stretches of time."

"I know. That part sucks, but I want to cover the stories shaping and impacting the world."

"Dating across three continents could be challenging."

"Challenging? It would be impossible. I suck at relationships, and besides, no guy would ever put in the time or effort to make it work."

"I would." Demetri put a lot of thought into what he said next. He didn't want to scare Angela off, but he had to tell her what was in his heart. "As long as we're honest about our feelings and put each other first, we can survive anything, Angela. Even international time zones."

He felt her body tense. "Demetri, you're a great guy and last night was amazing, but that's all it was. One night. I'm not looking for anything serious."

"Are you sure about that?" Demetri lowered his mouth and slowly brushed his lips across hers. She giggled, which made him smile. "I think we'd make a great team."

"We want different things. You want a family, and I love the single life."

"No, you don't. That's just a cover you use to keep people away."

Lips pursed, she turned away and stared out into the darkness. "That's not true."

"I think it is."

"Well, you're wrong."

Feelings of guilt and regret quickly consumed him. He'd

said too much, pushed too hard, and now her wall was back up. To smooth things over, Demetri kissed her cheek, the tip of her earlobe and then her shoulder blade. "I've been in lust a lot, and like a few times, but I've never fallen this hard or this fast for anyone," he confessed. "You're special to me, Angela, and I want us to be exclusive."

"Demetri, that's crazy. We just met!"

He started to speak, but Angela spoke over him.

"Let's just see what happens. No pressure, no expectations, no promises, okay?"

"Is there someone else?" Demetri heard the tremor in his voice, but there was nothing he could do about it. He couldn't stomach the thought of Angela being with another man and didn't want to share her with anyone else. "Are you sleeping with other men?"

Angela slid a hand down his chest, gripped his erection and stroked it until it came to life. "Why would I need someone else when I have all this?"

Then she whipped off the blanket, climbed onto his lap and rode him until he climaxed.

Demetri thought about the bubble bath they took afterward. While stretched out in the tub, they chatted about his baseball career, his ongoing rehab for his injured shoulder and the stress of being a celebrity. Angela didn't talk much, but she did answer all of his questions honestly. Demetri knew she had a string of ex-boyfriends, guys she'd dumped as soon as things got serious, but he wasn't a hit-it-and-quit-it type of man. And deep in his heart he knew Angela was the one. The only one. The right one. He wouldn't push her, though. He couldn't risk Angela shutting him out. Not when he wanted her to be his girl.

The phone rang, pulling Demetri out of his thoughts. He checked the number on the screen and then hit the speaker button. "Hey, Nicco, what's up?" he asked, glancing at the video screen. His brother's eyes were bloodshot, and his rumpled suit looked as though it had seen better days. "You look like hell. Lost big at the casino again, huh?"

"No, a bunch of punks broke into the restaurant near Miami Beach and trashed the place." His voice was hoarse and sounded as if he had a cold. "There's over fifty thousand dollars' worth of damage, and the new security system I had installed last week was destroyed."

"Damn, bro, I'm sorry. What did the cops say? Do they have any leads?"

"Nothing yet. They promised to keep me posted, but I'm not holding my breath."

"Do you want me to come out there? I could fly down this afternoon."

"You sound just like Rafael. He's in Madrid on business, but he's ready to come down here and lead the police investigation himself!"

The brothers laughed.

"That's what we do. We stick together." Demetri leaned against the counter. "Just say the word and I'm there."

Nicco shook his head. "You can't come to Miami. You're filming your new Nike commercial with Rashawn 'The Glove' Bishop this week, remember? Rashawn and his wife, Yasmin, were at the restaurant a few nights ago, and he sounded real excited about it."

"It can always be rescheduled."

"Don't bother. I won't be around anyways. I'm going to Argentina for a few days."

"What's in Argentina?"

"You mean besides babes, sunshine and a guaranteed good time?" Nicco chuckled. "How are things in Chi-Town? Not still tripping about that Angela Kelly broad, I hope."

At the sound of her name, a grin exploded across Demetri's face. He glanced up at the ceiling, thoughts of their night together at the front of his mind. Angela was the closest thing to perfection, the only woman he'd ever met to stop him dead in his tracks. She knew who she was and what she wanted. And that was damn sexy. He'd been with a lot of women and thought he'd seen it all when it came to the bedroom, but nothing compared to making love to Angela. He loved the sounds she made in bed, loved how she screamed and lost control. And the force of her orgasm always triggered his own. They'd made love three times last night, but just thinking about her juicy, pink lips made him hunger for another taste.

"Damn, bro, what's going on? You're smiling like a kid in a candy store!"

"I guess you could say Angela and I finally came to a mutual agreement."

Nicco straightened in his chair and moved so close to the LCD screen that Demetri could see the dark worry lines under his hazel eyes. "Did this *agreement* involve getting buck naked and going at it on your pool table?" he asked, wetting his lips with his tongue. "Come on, D. Fess up. I want to know all the dirty details."

"I'll bring you up to speed next time you're in town," Demetri said smoothly. Angela was special to him, and he didn't want to discuss the intimate details of their relationship with his brother. At least not yet. "Have a good one, Nicco. Take it easy."

A sly grin claimed his lips. "Trust me, bro, I intend to. I have a thick, curvy honey waiting for me in my bedroom as we speak."

That makes two of us, Demetri thought, grinning, *but my girl's more than just a pretty face. She's the total package, and I'll move heaven and earth to make her mine.*

Angela tiptoed out of the master bedroom, closed the door behind her and glanced down the hall. It was empty. No maids, no Demetri in sight. Spending the rest of the day in bed with Demetri was tempting, but Angela knew it was time to go. The party was over, and she didn't want to overstay her welcome. Besides, she had to meet her father at noon and didn't want to show up in rumpled clothes and with tangled hair. She owed her dad an apology for skipping the Globetrotters game last night and hoped he'd had fun with Rodney. Angela checked her watch. If she hustled, she could make a quick pit stop at home for a shower and a wardrobe change.

Clutching her purse to her chest, she headed down the hallway, careful not to make a sound. Angela didn't know where Demetri was, but she sensed it was the perfect time to make a clean getaway. He was probably hiding out in his media room, anxiously waiting for her to leave. There would be no terse exchanges or awkward goodbyes, and if she was lucky, she'd make it out of the house without seeing any of his staff or family members.

Her heart pounded as she crept down the staircase and through the grand sun-drenched foyer. Angela had a hand on the doorknob and a foot out the door when she heard Demetri call her name. Guilt pricked her heart and burned her skin with shame. She turned around, fully prepared to repeat the lie she'd rehearsed while upstairs getting dressed. But when she saw Demetri standing in the kitchen, holding a silver tray in his hands, she swallowed the fib.

"Where are you rushing off to?"

"Who, me?" Angela wanted to kick herself. *Of course he's talking to me!* They were the only two people in the foyer, and worse, he was staring right at her. "I'm going to get out of your hair. I bet you have appointments and interviews and a million other things to do today."

"I have nothing planned, besides spending the day with you."

A smile pinched her lips. It was hard being this close to Demetri, impossible to withstand the heat of his gaze and his boyish grin. Her feelings were all mixed up, and her hormones were raging out of control. If her body got any hotter she was going to faint.

"I made breakfast," he said, holding up the silver tray. "Do you like waffle paninis?"

"Waffle what? I've never heard of it."

"Then you're in for a treat because I made you an authentic Italian breakfast."

Angela stood in the doorway, her eyes wide and her mouth open. This was not what she'd expected to find when she came downstairs. Demetri Morretti had cooked for her—again. He stood there staring at her with such warmth and affection that she didn't have the heart to disappoint him. "Okay, I'll stay for breakfast," she said, closing the front door, "but after we eat I really have to go. I have, um, things to do."

"Do you mind if we eat in the living room? My favorite show is about to start."

"You're a big fan of *The Girls Next Door,* aren't you?" Angela teased. "I knew it."

"No, today's the start of celebrity week on *Family Feud,* and my old teammate is on."

"I love that show," Angela said with a laugh.

"What are we waiting for? Let's go watch the Feud!"

Entering the living room, Angela admired the dark couches, marble structures and the entertainment unit filled with the latest high-tech gadgets. But what stunned Angela were all of the towering built-in bookshelves. The estate had a two-story wine cellar, a bowling alley and a game room twice the size of her house, but Angela never dreamed Demetri would have more books than the Chicago public library. "You like to read?"

"Not like, *love.*" Demetri put the silver breakfast tray down on the glass coffee table. "If you think this is nice, wait until I show you the reading room."

"The reading room? Sounds intriguing. I'd love to see it."

"Right now?"

"Sure. Why not?"

"But what about breakfast?" His expression was thoughtful. "We were up late last night. Aren't you hungry?"

"No." Angela hid a self-incriminating grin. "I hope you don't mind, but I helped myself to some of the snacks in the mini bar."

Demetri chuckled. "As long as you didn't eat the last Snickers bar, we're good."

"Now you tell me!" Angela giggled.

He slipped an arm around her waist and led her down the hall. "This is my favorite room in the house," he said, entering the spacious, wide den. "I spend more time here than anywhere else."

The room was filled with padded chairs and antique reading lamps. Angela ambled over to one of the shelves and drew her index finger along the books in the row. Demetri owned all of the greats—Hemingway, Steinbeck and Faulkner—and had the most impressive collection of African-American literature she had ever seen.

Angela stood in stunned silence. Nothing made sense. The pieces of the puzzle didn't fit, and the more she tried to figure Demetri out, the more confused she was. Bad boys didn't garden or cook or read classic books. And they never, ever professed their love. But Demetri had. His words played in her mind now, but she pushed them aside and continued perusing the shelves. Angela didn't want to offend him, but she couldn't resist asking Demetri the question on the tip of her tongue. "Do you actually read these books, or are they here just for show?"

"I'm more than just a baseball player, Angela. That's what I do, not who I am."

"Then who are you?"

"An honest, loyal guy who loves beautiful things, beautiful places and strong, beautiful women who aren't afraid to speak their mind." Demetri touched a hand to her face, stroking her cheek with the tip of his thumb. "There are a couple things we need to clear up."

His caress sent a quiver through her, and for a moment she couldn't speak.

"I didn't storm into your studio for kicks, Angela. Your *Athletes Behaving Badly* piece was poorly written and full of lies."

"Lies?" she repeated, nailing him with a cold, hard look. "Name one."

"I never threw a beer bottle at that college kid in New Jersey."

"He said you did. Even pressed charges."

"It was one of my security guards, and as soon as I found out, I fired him," he explained in a firm tone. "I would never condone that type of behavior."

"Anything else I got wrong?"

Demetri nodded. "I never messed around with my teammate's wife, and I'm not the father of her baby, either. She made a pass at me at a white party in the Hamptons, but I shot her down."

"That's hard to believe."

"I'd never hook up with Lexus Washington. She's an ex-stripper who's screwed half the guys on my team. If I ever brought her home to my family, they'd disown me!"

Angela bit the bottom of her lip, looked away.

"I'm attracted to women like you. Classy, professional types who care about giving back and making a difference in our community."

"Don't make me out to be a saint, Demetri. I'm far from it."

"You are to me and to a lot of other people in this city." Demetri leaned into her. His lips touched her mouth. "I could get used to this, baby. You being here with me every day."

Angela didn't trust herself to speak. Not when her heart was racing and her feelings were a jumbled mess. But that was no surprise. She always found herself flustered when Demetri was around.

"I love you, baby, and I'm ready to commit to you."

"Love!" The word burst out of Angela's mouth and ricocheted around the den like machine-gun fire. "That's outrageous. We only met a few weeks ago, and besides, we're just kicking it, just having fun."

"There's no time limit on love," he murmured, brushing his lips against the slope of her ear. "When you know, you know, and there's no doubt in my mind that you're the woman I'm supposed to be with. No doubt at all. I'm all in, Angela. Ready to…"

Closing her eyes, she soaked in the beauty of the moment. His words resonated with her, filled her with a deep sense of peace. As he spoke, her temperature rose and her body grew hot. That always happened when Demetri touched her. The way he was stroking her arms and hips incited her passion. Blood roared through her veins. Her breasts enlarged, her nipples hardened, and the lips between her legs grew moist. Last night, their lovemaking had been wild, but right now, her desire for Demetri was stronger than ever.

Angela pressed her lips against Demetri's, kissing him slowly as if she was savoring the feel and taste of his mouth. Sliding a hand under his T-shirt, she stroked and caressed his shoulders and abs. But touching him wasn't enough. It didn't quench her body's thirst. Feasting on his mouth, she nibbled on his bottom lip, eagerly sucking and teasing his tongue.

Demetri trailed his lips along her earlobe, down her neck and across her shoulders. He wasn't shy about sharing his feelings or afraid to say what was on his mind. "You have no idea how amazing it feels being inside you," he whispered, slipping his hands under her dress and cupping her butt. "I'll never get tired of loving you, Angela. You'll never have to worry about anyone or anything coming between us."

Overtaken by desire and moved by his sweet, earnest

words, Angela crushed her lips against his mouth. Sliding a hand inside his dark-wash blue jeans, she stroked the length of his erection. Her passion was through the roof. And when Demetri slid a finger inside her, she shivered. His stroke fueled her desire, infected her body with an undeniable hunger.

Angela couldn't take any more. She wanted to feel Demetri inside her, loving her only the way he could. Burning up from head to toe, she felt sweat trickle down her face and back. They were stuck together, but the warmth of Demetri's hard body only increased her desire.

Demetri took a condom out of his pocket, protected himself and plunged so deep inside her that she collapsed against him. Winded, she fought to catch her breath, to stay in the moment. He gave her what she wanted and more.

Bracing herself against the nearby window, she draped her hands around his neck and hiked a leg around his waist. They moved together as one, like dancers gliding across the stage.

Suddenly her orgasm slammed into her with the force of a category-five hurricane. And by the time Demetri scooped her up in his arms and carried her upstairs to the master bedroom, Angela was no longer thinking about leaving the estate. So desperate to make love again, she couldn't stop fantasizing about all the salacious things she was going to do to Demetri in his Jacuzzi.

Chapter 15

"I hate to toot my own horn, but toot, toot!" Remy shrieked, wearing a wide, toothy smile that made her eyes twinkle. "You look like a million bucks, girlfriend!"

Leaning forward in her leather swivel chair, Angela inspected her hair and makeup in the lit oval mirror. "Thanks, Remy. As usual you did a great job."

"I know!" Winking, Remy snatched her jean jacket off the silver coat hook and slipped it on over her orange Bob Marley tank top. "I'll catch you later. I have to be at Glamour Girlz by six, and it's already ten to. Have a great show, girlfriend. Knock 'em dead!"

Sitting in her chair, alone in WJN-TV's cool, bright makeup room, Angela wondered if it was too late to back out of co-hosting the live morning show. How could she go on the air when she was a nervous wreck? At times like this, when Angela was scared and stressed-out, she would usually call her dad. But he was en route to Nashville.

Fidgeting with her bracelet, she restlessly crossed and uncrossed her legs. Outside in the hallway, Angela heard loud footsteps, the security alarm beeping in earnest and high-pitched voices. The room smelled of freshly squeezed lemons, and her favorite Wynton Marsalis song was playing on the radio, but it did little to relax her. Her stomach was twisted in a knot so tight, Angela feared she was going to be sick.

I should have never agreed to fill in for Earl, she thought, wiping her clammy palms along the side of her black fitted pencil skirt. *What if I trip over my words or misread the teleprompter? Those bloggers from Gossip News will crucify me online!*

Angela pressed her eyes shut. In the darkness, she saw Demetri's face, heard his quiet, soothing voice in her ear. These days she thought of the gorgeous baseball star and nothing else. Last Saturday was supposed to be a onetime thing, a mere night of carnal pleasure. But since their first date, they'd made love on four other occasions. Five, if she counted the quickie they'd had on Wednesday night in the front seat of his tinted Mercedes-Benz SUV. Angela knew she had to stop sneaking around with Demetri, but every time he called and invited her over, she caved. It was hard not to. He was thoughtful and caring and gave her the freedom to be herself—her true, authentic self—not the person she pretended to be in front of the cameras. They were goofy together and had laughed so much while volunteering at the Cook County Food Bank that the other volunteers poked fun at them.

Being with Demetri had become addictive. She had to talk to him and see him every day. It didn't matter how late it was or how stressful her day had been; she was never too tired to make the hour-long drive out to his home. Seeing Demetri made everything better. And when they were in bed, making love, moving together in perfect sync, Angela was in heaven. Nothing else mattered or compared to the euphoria she felt when Demetri was buried deep inside her, whispering soft words in her ears.

A smile appeared across Angela's face when she thought about the unexpected surprise she'd received hours earlier. When she'd stumbled into her office that morning—after spending the night with Demetri—and seen dozens of vases filled with yellow tulips and bunches of helium balloons hanging from the ceiling, she'd let out a shriek. Her coworkers had come running. Everyone had squealed and cheered and told her how lucky she was to have found a sweet, romantic guy.

Angela agreed, admitted they were right. Everything in the gift basket was dainty and heart-shaped, but what touched Angela the most was the personalized, handwritten card from Demetri. He'd written her words of encouragement, and as Angela sat in her makeup chair, his words came back to her and slowly soothed her troubled mind.

Her cell phone rang, blaring her current favorite pop song through the room. Angela scooped her cell off the makeup table and immediately pressed it to her ear. The only person who would call this early was Simone. "Simone, what are you doing up this early? Raiding the fridge again?"

"I'm not Simone, but I *am* raiding the fridge!"

"Demetri?"

"Your one and only."

Angela checked the time on the wall clock above the oval mirror. "What are you doing up so early? It's only six-fifteen."

"You're cohosting the morning show, and I didn't want to miss it," he said, his tone full of excitement. "Ready for your big debut?"

"I thought I was, but now that it's almost showtime, I'm scared to death."

"Baby, you're going to do great."

"But what if I don't? What if my nerves get the best of me and I screw up on live TV?"

"It's not going to happen. You're smart and articulate, and you think fast on your feet. Don't worry. You've got this."

His words made her smile, but the butterflies in her stomach remained.

"Did you get the gift basket?"

"Yes, it was waiting in my office when I arrived. Thanks, Demetri. I shared the bottle of champagne and the edible roses with my colleagues, and now they all love me!"

"I'm not surprised. You're easy to love, not to mention gorgeous, intelligent and..."

Angela felt a tickle emerge in her throat. The times when

Demetri talked about his feelings and their relationship, Angela wanted to cry. She knew they would never be able to have a real future and share a life together.

An idea came to her, but she dismissed it when her doubts quickly flooded in. Telling Demetri about her past, about the wild and crazy things she'd done during her college days, was not an option. Not today, not ever. The risk of hurting him was too great.

"What time do you finish up today?"

"Three o'clock, maybe four. It depends on how long my afternoon meeting goes."

"When you wrap up, there'll be a town car waiting out front to bring you to my estate," he explained. "I have the whole day planned. We'll have a special celebratory lunch, play a round or two of golf, then watch the new James Bond movie in my home theater."

Angela frowned. "But that movie isn't out until November."

"I know, but since you're a huge Daniel Craig fan, I asked my manager to get it."

"Just like that?"

Demetri chuckled. "Yeah, baby, just like that."

"Wow, it must be nice having friends in high places."

"Only if it helps me get closer to you," he said, his voice soft and earnest. "I love having you here with me. If I had my way, you'd be living here permanently."

Growing up, her dad had never shared his thoughts or emotions, and over time Angela had adopted his passive approach in relationships. So instead of responding to what Demetri had just said, she changed the subject. "It's going to be gorgeous outside today. We should get out, maybe check out one of the music festivals?"

"I wish we could, but it's just not worth the hassle. We're better off staying in," he said. "I went to the grocery store late last night, and if not for my security guards, I'd still be in the produce section, fighting my way through the crowd."

"So, what are you going to do? Spend the rest of the summer holed up in your house?"

"Pretty much. I have everything I need at home, and since I schedule most of my meetings and appointments here at the estate, there's really no reason to go out."

"Oh, I know what this is about," she said, trying hard not to laugh. "You're strapped for cash and can't afford to take me out. Don't worry, baby. It's my treat!"

Demetri roared with laughter. "Where do you want to go?"

"I don't know. Let's jump on the L line and see where it takes us."

"Angela, we can't. I need to let my team know what we're doing beforehand so they can make the necessary arrangements."

"What arrangements, Demetri? It's not that serious. We don't have to go to a fancy restaurant or an upscale club. As long as we're together, I'm happy."

"Okay, then I'll have my assistant reserve Philander's for us. We can have a nice romantic dinner alone, then dance to the live jazz band."

"We don't need the entire restaurant, Demetri. Just one table." Angela slid off her chair and inspected her appearance in the mirror. The cropped, white blazer fit her curves just right, and her turquoise-hued accessories made the entire outfit pop. She sat back down in the chair and said, "The whole point of going out is to interact with other people, so let's just stroll around downtown and see where the night takes us."

"Maybe you're right. Maybe we should get out and do something different."

"Maybe?" she sassed. "Baby, I'm *always* right."

"Except when it comes to making breakfast. The entire house still smells like smoke!"

Angela giggled. "Hey, that's not my fault. *You're* the one

who wanted to have a quickie. I tried to stop you, but you just wouldn't listen—"

Salem stuck her head in the door and waved.

"I have to go," Angela said. "I'll see you later, okay?"

"For sure. Have a great show, beautiful. I'll be watching!"

Angela ended the call, slipped her cell phone back into her purse and turned to her boss.

"Are you all right?" Salem wore a concerned expression on her face. "You don't look too good, and we're live in fifteen minutes."

Angela swallowed. It was here. The moment she'd been waiting for her entire life. Her big break, the opportunity to show her producers she was more than just a pretty face. She replayed Demetri's words in her head. *You're smart and articulate, and you think fast on your feet. Don't worry. You've got this.*

Her breathing slowed, her hands stopped shaking, and the butterflies fluttering around in her stomach slowed. Angela smiled and hopped to her feet. "I'm great. Couldn't be better."

"Ready to head into the studio? Everyone's waiting."

"You bet your stiletto boots I am!"

Laughing, Salem led Angela down the bright, narrow hallway. On the walls were framed pictures of world leaders, prominent figures and the station's most celebrated reporters. Angela felt her confidence rise. One day, she'd be an acclaimed reporter, interviewing influential people and traveling all over the world. A question sneaked up on her, one that brought her thoughts back to Demetri. *Was he serious about us having a long-distance relationship? Would he really come visit me if I lived abroad?*

"I don't know how you did it, Angela, but convincing Demetri's brothers to join him on *Eye on Chicago* next month was a brilliant idea," Salem said, her tone one of awe.

Angela snapped out of her thoughts and gave her boss a grateful smile. "Thanks, but to be honest, it didn't take much convincing at all. Demetri called, and they agreed, just like that."

"The Morretti brothers are the hottest bachelors in the world, and since posting the details of the interview on Twitter and Facebook, I've received hundreds of messages."

"I'm not surprised. These days they're more popular than ever."

"Think they'll agree to do a fun *Love Connection*–type game?"

"I bet they'd love that, especially Nicco. He's a real ladies' man."

"That's what I heard." Salem winked. "That's not all I heard. I read online this morning in *Celebrity Scoop* that you and Demetri Morretti are lovers."

Angela gave a shaky laugh. "Those online publications will say anything to attract readers."

"I know. That's what I thought, until I saw the pictures."

"What pictures?"

"There you are. I've been looking all over for you!" The associate producer, a stout Polish man with fleshy cheeks, rushed over and grabbed Angela around the waist. "No time to waste! We're live in sixty seconds!"

Chapter 16

Madison's Steak Bar, a popular restaurant in the heart of downtown Chicago, was packed with chic, fashionable patrons every night of the week. Tables were close, only an arm's length away, but diners didn't seem to mind. Conversations were loud and spirited, and laughter flowed freely around the cathedral-shaped dining room. Crystal chandeliers, milk-white carpets and cozy booths gave the space an old-world feel, one that fit the mellow atmosphere perfectly.

"Want the last bite?" Demetri held out his spoon. His eyes were glued to Angela's lips, and he wore a devilish grin on his lean, handsome face. "This is the holy grail of gelato, baby. It doesn't get much better than this!"

Leaning forward, Angela parted her lips and slowly sucked the rich, creamy dessert off of his silver spoon. "You're right. That's good."

"I'm glad you suggested this place. It's nice, and everyone here is real chill."

"My dad and I used to come here all the time. We'd eat, watch the game and talk and laugh for hours," she said, a wistful expression on her face. "He's a long-distance truck driver, so I don't get to see him much, but when I do, it's just like old times."

"The next time your dad's in town, I'd like to meet him."

"Why?"

"Because I'm hot for his daughter, and I plan to be around for a *very* long time."

Angela giggled and shook her head incredulously. "Demetri, you're crazy."

"Not crazy, just grateful to have a second lease on life." His demeanor was calm but his gaze was intense. "I'm just a regular guy who fell in love with an extraordinary girl who completes me in every way."

"Stop playing around."

"I'm not playing, Angela. I mean every word." He touched a hand to her cheek. "I have everything a man could want. Wealth, fame, more money than I could spend in this lifetime. The only thing missing from my life was you."

His cell phone rang, but he didn't touch it. Instead, Demetri continued stroking and caressing her skin. Angela loved when he did that. He looked right at her when he spoke, no matter what he was doing or what was going on around him. He always gave her his undivided attention. Angela liked everything Demetri was saying, and she felt the same way, but she couldn't return the sentiment. Not because she didn't love him, but because the risk was too great. If Demetri ever found out about her past, he'd dump her like yesterday's trash. And she'd never be able to survive his rejection. It was better that they just hung out and had fun, rather than get serious. But when Angela told Demetri that, the smile slid off his face.

"What are you saying? That you don't see us together for the long term?"

Angela opened her mouth, but a booming male voice spoke over her.

"Sign this to Hakeem," the speaker barked. A scrawny, middle-aged black man with tattoo-covered arms tossed a receipt down on the table. "And I'll need a picture with you, too."

Demetri kept his eyes on Angela but spoke to the dark-haired stranger in the wrinkled Chicago Royals jersey. "Now's not a good time. I'm talking to my girl. Come back in an hour."

"Just hurry up and sign it. I don't have all day. I'm about to get up out of here."

"Then leave. No one's stopping you."

"I told my son I'd get your autograph, and I'm not leaving without it." The man pressed his palms down on the table, getting right up in Demetri's face. His fast, heavy breathing filled the air, and his booming voice attracted the attention of patrons dining nearby.

In seconds, there was a crowd gathered around the booth. Cell phones flashed in Demetri's face and the dining room was abuzz with excited chatter. "Signing this receipt is the least you could do," the stranger snarled, baring his teeth. "You played like crap last season. Hell, I've seen Little Leaguers play better!"

Demetri shot to his feet. The veins in his neck were throbbing, his hands were curled into fists, and his eyes were dark with rage. Angela stood and wrapped an arm around his waist. "Baby, let's go. He's not worth it."

"Chump, scram before I make you a knuckle sandwich to go."

Angela recognized the voice behind them, and when Rodney elbowed his way through the crowd and stepped forward, she felt a mixture of relief and apprehension. Her kid brother was a foot taller than the belligerent stranger and outweighed him by at least fifty pounds. The expression on Rodney's face could scare the Devil, and when he folded his broad arms across his muscled chest, the man gulped.

"Never mind," the stranger said, backing away from the booth. "You're not my son's favorite baseball player anyways. Jeter is."

The crowd dispersed, diners returned to their seats, and by the time the busty female manager hustled over, the dining area had returned to normal.

"Thanks, kid. What's your name?"

"Rodney Kelly."

Demetri glanced at Angela and then gave a slow nod. "It's good to meet you, Rodney. I've heard a lot about you."

"Only half of it's true. My sister exaggerates!"

"Rodney, what are you doing here?" Angela demanded, sitting back down in the booth.

"I came to see you."

"Now's not a good time."

Shaking his head, he threw his hands up in the air. "When is? I've been trying to get ahold of you for weeks, but you won't return my calls. We need to talk."

"I have nothing to say to you."

"Fine," Rodney said. "I'll talk and you listen."

"You guys need some privacy." Demetri squeezed her hand, then lowered his mouth to her ear and dropped a kiss on her cheek. "I'll be back. Don't rush. Spend as much time as you need with your brother."

Angela started to protest, but Demetri strode off. Her eyes followed him through the dining room and off into the TV-filled lounge. He took a seat at the L-shaped bar and made himself at home among the other patrons who were chatting, sipping wine and cheering on the Royals.

"Have you been getting my messages?"

Angela nodded and stared absently out the window. Golden lights sparkled in the night. The view of the Chicago skyline was nothing short of spectacular. Angela wished Demetri was beside her instead of her brother. Rodney was trouble, and she suspected he'd tracked her down to hit her up for money. Again.

"I'm sorry I took—"

"Don't you mean *stole?*" she said, cutting him off. "You betrayed my trust, Rodney, and I don't know if I'll ever be able to forgive you."

He drew up a chair, straddled it and sat down. "I didn't know what else to do, Angela. I was desperate and I needed the money fast."

"For what? To buy drugs?"

"Drugs?" A frown jammed between his thick, dark eyebrows. "I don't sell or use drugs. Never have, never will. That's not my speed."

"Then what did you steal the money for?"

Rodney stared up at the potted lights and then down at his big, beefy hands. "I—I—I took the money to pay off a bookie," he blurted out. "I bet on the Indy 500 and lost big. Icepick said if I didn't pay up he'd hurt Pops, and I got... scared."

"Why didn't you tell me?"

"I couldn't. I'm always screwing up, and I didn't want to let you or Pops down again. But I'm going to pay you back every penny of that money, sis. I swear."

"How, when you don't have a job and spend all day hanging out with your friends?"

"I don't kick it on the block anymore," he said. "Dad let me move back in if I promised to straighten up, and I've been searching for work all week."

Angela didn't speak, just nodded her head. She saw Demetri, sitting alone at the bar, and smiled when he glanced her way. He wore a concerned expression. She thought about the things he'd told her about his family, about all the messed-up things his relatives had done to him over the years. They'd sold him out to the tabloids, applied for credit cards in his name and pilfered items from his estate when they thought no one was looking. He'd forgiven each one, no questions asked. "You can't choose your relatives or decide who is worthy enough to share your last name," he'd said one afternoon while basking by his Olympic-size pool. "Your family is God's gift to you, *even* the crazy ones, and you're supposed to love them no matter what."

His words played in her mind now, but Angela still wasn't ready to forgive Rodney.

"I better let you get back to your date. Your man's been sitting at the bar a long time."

"Demetri's not my man. We're just…just hanging out."

Gesturing to the bar with a flick of his bald head, he broke into a grin that revealed his dimples. "Does he know that? Because he looks mighty sprung to me," he said, raising his eyebrows. "He's not watching the game. He's watching you!"

"Demetri and his brothers are doing my show next month. We just came down here to discuss the details of the interview." She could tell by the look on Rodney's face that he didn't believe her. Angela wasn't surprised. She didn't believe the words coming out of her mouth, either. Their relationship was different from anything she'd ever experienced before, but Angela wasn't going to tell her brother or anyone else that she was in love with Demetri. "We have a good time together, but it's nothing serious."

"That's too bad. I thought I was finally going to have a brother-in-law and some nieces and nephews to spoil and shoot hoops with!"

"Don't worry, Rodney. I'm working on it."

Angela's face held a serious expression, but inside she felt downright giddy.

"My man!" Her brother jumped to his feet and bumped fists with Demetri. "Now, that's what I'm talking about!"

Her cheeks burned red when Demetri slid back into the booth and draped an arm over her shoulders. He whispered in her ear in a sexy tone that caused desire to consume her body. Then he lowered his mouth to her lips. She tilted her chin and kissed him back.

"We should all hang out sometime." Demetri fixed his gaze on Angela but spoke to her brother. "Rodney, are you as crazy about the Royals as your sister is?"

"Naw, basketball's more my sport."

"Cool. Maybe we can check out a play-off game."

"Sounds good." Rodney took his cop-style sunglasses out

of the side pocket of his faded, blue jeans and slid them on. "I have to go. I have a job interview tomorrow, and I have a hell of a time waking up in the morning."

"I hear you, man. If it wasn't for your sister, I'd stay in bed until one o'clock!"

The men chuckled.

"'Bye," Rodney said, flashing two fingers, and then he turned and strode off.

Demetri took out his wallet, dropped several hundred-dollar bills on the leather billfold and grabbed his jacket. "Rodney, hold up. I think I'm going to need your help."

"To do what?" he asked, a quizzical expression on his face.

Demetri pointed at the front window. A group of twenty-somethings, holding their cell phones in the air, stood pressed against the glass, frantically snapping pictures. "Think you can clear a path from the front door to my Bentley?"

Rodney grinned and puffed out his chest. "You don't even have to ask."

Chapter 17

Demetri settled into his favorite leather chair and propped his size-twelve feet up on the chocolate-brown ottoman. He had a glass of Veneto in one hand and the remote control in the other. Demetri couldn't recall the last time he felt this relaxed, this happy.

The French doors, leading out onto the deck, were open, allowing the intoxicating scents and sounds of spring to fill his game room. Autographed baseball jerseys were displayed on the navy blue walls, barstools and low-hanging pub lights gave the space a cool, sophisticated feel, and the multicolored area rugs complemented the decor perfectly. Demetri owned every arcade machine known to man, dozens of table games and had over ten thousand video games in his collection.

Demetri turned on the ninety-inch wall-mounted TV, and when a commercial for *Eye on Chicago* came on, a grin exploded onto his mouth. These days, that was all he seemed to do. Eating breakfast with Angela in bed, watching the sunset on his balcony and luxuriating in his Jacuzzi was all it took to make him break out in an ear-to-ear smile.

Taking a sip of his wine, he cast a glance at his team. Todd was sitting at the bar, devouring his second bowl of penne, Lloyd was reviewing the terms of his new five-year Gatorade contract, and Nichola was typing on her beloved iPad. Demetri didn't want to kick them out, but it was time to bring their weekly meeting to a close. He wanted to be showered and changed by the time Angela arrived for their date. Though, if she wanted to join him in the shower he wouldn't mind. His grin doubled in length at the thought of making love to her in the middle of the afternoon.

For the past three weeks, he'd spent all of his free time with Angela, and when they were apart, she was all he could think of. It wasn't until meeting Angela that he realized how empty his life was. For years, he'd stumbled through life, searching for its meaning, its purpose. He loved playing baseball, had a great family and legions of loyal fans around the world, but he'd always longed for more. He had craved something deeper than just fame and fortune. Demetri wanted someone to share his life with, someone he could trust, and one warm, fateful day he'd found her.

Angela's love had changed him, restored his faith in people. Angela loved to socialize, found beauty in the smallest things in life and always had a smile. Nothing got her down—not her critics, not her hypercritical producers, not even the sexist male crew she worked with. Open-minded and always up for a good time, she thrived on trying new things and living in the moment. Demetri admired the way she carried herself and her zest for life. Being with Angela reminded him of the time—before fame and fortune came calling—when he was a fun, outgoing guy who didn't have a care in the world.

"That's the best damn penne I've ever had," Todd announced, leaning back into his chair and patting his stomach. "Thanks, Demetri. I owe you one."

Demetri snapped out of his thoughts and nodded at his agent.

"We've hit a roadblock in our plans for the Fourth of July extravaganza," Nichola announced, plopping down in the chair beside him. "I met with Claudia Jeffries-Medina and the director of the recreation center yesterday, and she shot down all of our ideas. We told her the Fourth of July extravaganza is for underprivileged kids, but she didn't seem to care."

"That's a bummer." Lloyd tossed his files into his briefcase, locked it and rested it on the floor. "You win some, you lose some, I guess."

"You can say that again. It's been one setback after another, and I'm starting to think we should postpone the event."

"How many families were you planning to invite?"

"This has been a major bone of contention," Nichola explained, combing a hand through her hair. "I wanted to make this a huge, over-the-top bash, but the hall can only accommodate two hundred people, and the director is dead set against having tents on the property."

Demetri raised an eyebrow. "Two hundred people? That's it? No offense, Nichola, but that doesn't sound like much of a party to me."

"Find somewhere else to have the fundraiser," Lloyd suggested, taking off his eyeglasses and cleaning them with his white silk handkerchief. "There are plenty of recreation centers in and around the Chicago area that can accommodate larger numbers."

Nichola sighed. "It's too late to find another venue. The fundraiser is only weeks away."

"Then we'll have it here."

His team exchanged quizzical looks.

"Here where?" Todd asked, his lean, tanned face screwed up into a frown.

"Here at the estate."

Eyes popped, jaws dropped, and foreheads wrinkled.

"No way." Lloyd gave an adamant shake of his head. "It's too risky."

"I agree. These kids come from bad, crime-ridden neighborhoods, and—"

Demetri drained his wineglass and put it on the side table. "Todd, relax. Everything will be fine. If something breaks, it can always be replaced."

"I'm not worried about something breaking," he mumbled. "I'm worried about those badass kids robbing you blind!"

"Having the Fourth of July extravaganza here is a wonderful idea. Imagine all the great press we'll get!" Clapping her hands together, Nichola whooped for joy. "And as long as the weather cooperates, we can set up everything outside."

A sly grin fell across Todd's mouth. "I like your way of thinking. Keep the runts and their thieving parents *far, far* away from the house."

Demetri glared at his agent but spoke warmly to his publicist. "Nichola, you're the best. I don't know what I'd do without you."

Her eyes lit up. "You don't have to thank me. You know I'll do anything for you."

"I know, but still. Just wanted you to know I appreciate all of your hard work." Resting the remote control on the ottoman, he swiped up his cell phone and stood. "I'm going upstairs. Feel free to eat and drink as much as you want."

"Where are you rushing off to?" Nichola asked, crossing her legs. "I thought we were staying in and watching old Al Pacino movies on TV."

"Can't. I'm taking Angela to Jazz Fest."

Lloyd scratched his head. "Jazz Fest? All the way up in Freeport? But you hate crowds."

"And road trips!" Nichola added.

"Yeah, but Angela is a huge Wynton Marsalis fan, and he's performing there tonight."

Todd pointed a finger at Demetri. "Have fun, but make sure your security guards take all the necessary precautions to keep you guys safe."

"I gave the guards the night off. I want to be alone with Angela."

"Are you sure that's a good idea?" Lloyd questioned, straightening in his chair. "I know you'll be wearing a disguise, but if someone recognizes you, all hell could break loose."

"No disguise tonight. I need to look fly as hell when I'm

out with Angela. She's gorgeous and I don't want to look like a scrub beside her!"

The guys chuckled, agreeing fervently.

"I almost forgot," Nichola said, her tone apologetic. "I told the Kids Awards you're not interested in being a presenter, but do you want—"

"I wish you would have spoken to me first before refusing the invitation."

"Why? Every year they invite you, and every year you turn them down."

"I know," Demetri said, "but this year I'd like to go. It might be fun."

Three sets of eyes stared incredulously at him.

Todd picked up his empty wineglass and sniffed it. "Someone must have drugged your Veneto, because you're talking crazy."

"One last thing before we wrap up," Lloyd said, sliding off his barstool. "My wife wants to know what time to expect you guys on Memorial Day. After last year's debacle, she decided to have invitations made and wants to have a general consensus before having them printed."

"Tell Trudy I'm sorry, but I won't be able to make it."

"Why not? You always spend Memorial Day with us."

"I'm taking Angela to Venice for the weekend," he explained, wearing a proud smile. "We're taking the Morretti family jet, and I've already booked the Ruzzini Palace, a driver and an English-speaking tour guide to show us all of the sights."

Nichola's face crumpled. "You're taking her to Italy for the weekend? That's insane! And ridiculously expensive!"

"Angela's worth it. She means a lot to me and…" Demetri broke off speaking, stopping himself from gushing like a love-struck teenager. Morretti men didn't sweat females, and if his brothers ever found out he was head over heels for Angela— the woman who'd dissed him on national television—they'd tease him mercilessly. "These last few months with Angela have been incredible, and it's about time I wined her and dined her. Venice is one of the most romantic cities in the world, and I plan to make it a weekend she'll never forget."

"Wow, you're going all out." Todd whistled loudly.

"If you guys move any faster, you'll be married by Christmas!"

I'd like nothing more. The thought gave Demetri pause. Not because getting married after a three-month-long courtship was crazy, but because he'd never considered proposing to anyone before. But from the moment he first laid eyes on Angela, he knew deep down that she was as exquisite as a white diamond. And everything she'd said and done since their first date made him love and respect her even more. He liked having Angela right by his side, and the thought of spending the rest of his life with her didn't scare him; it filled him with pride.

"You know she's only using you to boost the ratings of her stupid show, right?" Nichola snorted. "I know her type. She'll do anything to stay on top."

"She isn't using me, Nichola—"

"Yes, she is! Open your eyes!" His publicist sounded worried, as if she was on the verge of tears. "Angela's dated dozens of pro athletes, and once you do her show, she'll dump you and move on to the next star. That's how she is. That's how she operates."

Demetri tried to remain calm, tried to act as though her words didn't faze him, but they did. They stung, burned like hell. His biggest fear was that Angela would leave him for someone else or that she'd choose fame and stardom over him. Nichola's comments just fueled his doubts.

"Women like Angela Kelly only look out for themselves," Nichola continued, her tone ice-cold. "She isn't going to stick around for the long haul, and she definitely isn't wife material."

"I disagree." Todd tore his gaze away from the TV screen

and addressed Demetri. "I like her. She's smart and talented and not afraid to speak her mind. She'll tell you the truth, not just what you want to hear, and that speaks volumes about her character. Angela's definitely the type of woman you need in your—"

"Todd, what do you know?" Nichola spat, cutting him off. "You're hardly an expert when it comes to love and relationships. You've been married three times, and your last girlfriend dumped you for a gardener!"

He coughed and then scratched at his crooked nose. "Whatever. I might be unlucky in love, but I know a good woman when I see one. And Angela Kelly is one of the great ones."

"Thanks, man. I feel the same way. That's why I want Angela to meet my parents."

"Your parents!" his team shouted.

"What do you even know about her?" Nichola asked, now pacing the length of the game room. "I mean, besides the fact that she's on TV and that she's a good lay?"

"Don't," Demetri warned, his teeth clenched and his eyes narrowed. "Angela's special to me, and I won't let you or anyone else disrespect her."

A crooked smile crossed Nichola's face, one that darkened the shade of her eyes. "I know your parents and your family really well, Demetri. They're not going to like her."

"I think they will. Angela makes me happy, and that's all that matters."

"I thought you wanted to settle down, get married and have a bunch of kids?"

"I do, Lloyd. That hasn't changed."

"And Angela's down for that?" Todd asked, a quizzical expression on his face. "I'm a pretty good judge of character, and I don't see her swapping red-carpet events for breast-feeding and changing diapers."

"Maybe not right now, but in time she'll come around."

Nichola touched his forearm lightly. "Demetri, she's going

to hurt you. I just know it. She reminds me a lot of Shai, and…"

Demetri felt his body stiffen and all the muscles in his neck tense. He didn't want to think about his ex. The woman who had chosen fame and stardom over him. Whenever he heard one of her chart-topping pop songs on the radio, he wondered what could have been. Or at least he used to. Ever since meeting Angela, he'd forgotten about every other girl. Finally, after years of being lied to, used and deceived, he'd met a woman who thrilled him and completed him in every way.

"Oh, I'm sorry. I had no idea you had company."

At the sound of Angela's voice, Demetri cranked his head to the right. There, standing beside the French doors, was the woman who made his heart sing. Her knee-length leopard-print dress, which clung to her curves, looked amazing on her. And her sky-high heels showed off her long, toned legs.

Three long, quick strides and Demetri had Angela in his arms. "Baby, you hit it out of the ballpark tonight," he praised, looking her up and down. "I might have to bring my security detail with us to Freeport after all."

"You need to come down to my set more often," she quipped. "You're great for my ego!"

"Well, you're great for me, period." Unable to resist, Demetri crushed his lips against her soft, luscious mouth. Caressing her cheek, he kissed her thoroughly as if he had all the time in the world. Her perfume filled his nostrils with its rich fragrance and aroused his hunger and desire for her.

"Baby, your team's staring at us," she whispered, breaking off the kiss and smiling sheepishly. "And your publicist looks pissed. If looks could kill, I'd be six feet under."

"Never mind her," Demetri said, stealing another quick kiss. "Her favorite contestant got voted off *The Song* last night and she's been in a funk ever since!"

Angela giggled.

They strolled across the room with their fingers inter-twined.

"Hi, I'm Angela. It's great to meet you both."

Todd and Lloyd scrambled to their feet and almost tripped over each other in their haste to reach her first. After shaking hands and enjoying a few minutes of conversation with the guys, Angela waved at Nichola.

"It's good to see you," Angela said brightly. "How are things going?"

Nichola didn't smile or wave back. Instead she stood staring at them intently. Her eyes were narrowed, her arms were crossed, and she tapped her heeled foot impatiently on the floor. Demetri didn't know what her problem was, but he intended to find out. But before he could speak, Nichola said, "Angela, you're here, *again*—how nice."

Demetri shot Nichola a what-the-hell look, and she turned away.

"I'm out of here. See you guys later."

Within seconds, she packed up her things, grabbed her lightweight red coat and left. Demetri was relieved to see her go, but when Lloyd and Todd made themselves at home on the couch and started asking Angela dozens of questions, his good mood fizzled. At this rate, they'd never leave! He tried to catch Todd's attention, but his agent was too busy making googly eyes at Angela. And Lloyd was no better. The happily married father of three had flushed cheeks, and every time he opened his mouth, he tripped over his words. Demetri had never seen him smile so wide or heard him laugh so loud.

"I don't mean to be rude, guys, but it's time for you to leave."

"Go shower and change. We'll keep Angela company while you're gone."

"Yeah," Todd agreed, eagerly nodding his head. "I want to hear all about her show."

"I got an idea." Demetri grabbed the leather briefcases beside the bar and shoved one into each of their hands and then gestured to the door. "Why don't you guys go home to your kids and significant others? Bet they're dying to see you."

Their faces fell and their shoulders slumped.

"Come on," Lloyd whined. "Angela was just about to tell us which Oscar-winning actor has a secret foot fetish!"

"You guys don't have to go home," Demetri said, trying hard not to laugh, "but you have to get the hell out of here... now!"

Chapter 18

Should I go for classy chic or sex kitten? Angela wondered as she cast a critical eye over the trendy designer dresses she was holding up under her chin. An hour after getting out of the shower, she was still standing in front of the mirror, stressing over what to wear. Dinner was simmering on the stove, scented candles had been lit and her favorite CD was playing on the living-room stereo. Soft, sensuous music filled the air, creating a romantic vibe that put Angela in a mood for slow dancing and passionate lovemaking. All she needed now was her man, and life would be perfect.

Her body warmed and flushed with heat at the thought of Demetri. Angela never imagined she'd ever claim a man as her own, let alone cook, clean and wax for him, but that was exactly what she'd done. Dating Demetri was an adventure, one filled with laughs, tender moments and toe-curling sex. And he was so ridiculously romantic. Angela went to bed every night with a smile on her face. But Demetri was more than just a great guy. He was everything she'd ever wanted in a man and more.

Angela's eyes drifted to the digital clock sitting on her dresser. She couldn't stop counting down the seconds until Demetri would arrive. Her behavior was juvenile, completely out of character, but these days Angela wasn't thinking like a mature woman; she was acting more like a love-struck teen. Since meeting Demetri, she'd become someone else. Someone her producers and crew seemed to like much better. Maybe it was because she smiled more and wasn't so up-tight about everything.

Or maybe, a little voice inside her head said, *you're happier because for the first time in your life you're being your authentic self.*

Pondering the thought, Angela realized it was true. Every day after taping *Eye on Chicago,* Angela jumped in her car, anxious and excited to meet up with Demetri, not fretting about her on-camera performance or what her critics would say. And since attending Jazz Fest in Freeport two weeks earlier, Demetri had taken her from one public event to the other. On Thursday they went to a movie premiere, the following afternoon they dropped the top on his Rolls-Royce Phantom and cruised down to the beach, and yesterday he'd surprised her with front-row tickets to see the Jabbawockeez. At the show, fans approached Demetri for pictures and autographs, but he didn't trip. He held babies, shook hands and smiled for the cameras. Angela loved seeing that side of him, loved watching him talk and laugh with his adoring fans.

Eyes wide with alarm, Angela cast a glance over her shoulder. She waited, listened intently. A loud crackling sound filled the air, and a thick, heavy mist drifted inside the bedroom. Chucking the dresses onto the bed, Angela tore down the hall and burst into the kitchen as if it was on fire. And it was. Smoke was rising out of the pots, and the stench of charred meat was suffocating. The smoke alarm wailed so loud, Angela's head throbbed.

Grabbing the frying pan with one hand and the stainless-steel pot with the other, she dumped them into the sink and turned the water on full blast. The pots fizzled as steam rose from the rubble. The blackened meat looked like rubber.

Angela threw open the window and took deep gulps of air. The sky was overcast, a dark, menacing shade of gray, and the wind was blowing hot and fast. After cleaning the stove and mopping the floor, Angela ambled over to the kitchen table and plopped down on a chair. Her hair was damp, her short silk robe smelled like charcoal, and sweat drenched her arms and legs.

Fanning a hand to her face, she stared at the gold wine flutes, the gleaming utensils and flickering candles. The plates were empty and would stay that way unless she could find a restaurant that would deliver. It was Friday night, the last day of classes for university students, and no doubt her favorite spots were jam-packed with inebriated graduates.

Angela glanced at the pantry, stocked to the brim with food, and smiled despite her frustration. Last Sunday, Demetri had shown up at her house with bags of groceries and whipped up a to-die-for Italian brunch. Maybe all wasn't lost, she thought, straightening in her seat. Maybe she could still surprise Demetri with a home-cooked meal. But what? Angela thought for a moment and came up empty. But she knew just whom to call. Simone was a whiz in the kitchen, and she'd know just what to do.

Confident she could salvage her romantic evening, Angela surged to her feet and swiped the cordless phone off the cradle. It was the perfect time to call. Jayden and Jordan were already in bed, and Simone and Marcus were probably relaxing on the couch, watching their favorite TV show. And if Simone came through for her, Angela was going to treat her to lunch. They hadn't been to the Skyline Grill in weeks, and they were overdue for a relaxing gabfest at their favorite hotspot.

"Hello?"

"Hey, girl," Angela said when Simone answered the phone. "What's up?"

"Who's this?"

"Quit playing. It's me."

"Me, who?"

Angela heard the edge in her tone and knew her friend was upset. And Angela knew why. "Sorry for not returning your calls," she began, leaning against the kitchen counter. "Things have been crazy the last few weeks. Between taping, volunteering at the shelter, doing the live morning show and—"

"Doing Demetri," she tossed out.

"Don't be like that, Simone. You know I'd never choose a guy over you."

"I've seen the tabloids. I know what's up."

Angela felt her face harden. "What's that supposed to mean?"

"You have a man now, so you ditched your girls. Even me, your best friend, and I'm eight months pregnant and swollen like a beach whale!"

"You're right, Simone. I haven't been a very good friend lately. Do you forgive me?"

"I will if you babysit the boys next Friday," she quipped, giggling.

"Sure, no problem. They can spend the whole weekend with me," Angela said, sighing in relief. "Every time we talk, you're planning another trip. Where are you and Marcus going now?"

"To a couples spa in Las Vegas." Her tone brightened with excitement. "Girl, I need some R & R in the worst way. And some cute new maternity clothes, too, because nothing in my closet fits anymore!"

The friends laughed.

"Simone, I need your help."

"Sure, no problem. What's up?"

"I burned dinner."

"What else is new?" Simone joked. "You *always* burn dinner."

In the background, Angela heard someone chuckle and knew Simone's husband, Marcus, was listening in. "Today was Demetri's last day at the Sports Rehab Clinic," she explained, drumming her fingertips absently on the counter.

"I wanted to surprise him with a home-cooked meal, but the steaks just went up in flames."

"Do what you always do," Simone advised. "Order in from an expensive restaurant, put the food on your favorite set of china and pretend you slaved over a hot stove for hours."

"I can't do that again. Not tonight," she argued. Angela's gaze drifted to the sink, her shoulders slumped in defeat. "I want to do something special for Demetri, something he'd never expect."

"Answer the door buck naked!"

Angela cracked up, but when she heard the doorbell chime, she killed her laughter. "Gotta go. Demetri's here!"

"Have fun, girlfriend. Rock his world!"

Hustling out of the kitchen, spraying air freshener as she went, Angela rushed down the hall and reached the foyer in ten seconds flat. At the thought of seeing him, a girlish smile exploded across her face. The night wasn't ruined. She could still do something special for Demetri. She'd treat him to dinner at his favorite restaurant, then spring for the penthouse suite at Trump International Hotel and Tower. Demetri loved it there, and so did she. *We can play dirty card games again,* she thought. *And this time, I'll let him win!*

The doorbell chimed. Again and again.

Angela whipped off her robe, dropped it at her feet and slipped on her leopard-print sandals. Checking herself out in the mirror, Angela decided she'd never looked sexier. Her eyes were bright, her skin was glowing, and her thick hair was a wild, tousled mess.

A smirk pinched her crimson-red lips. That was just the look she was going for—bold, brazen, down for anything. But when Angela opened the front door and saw Nichola standing on her porch, her smile froze. "Hey," she said, shielding herself with the door. "Um, what's up?"

"We need to talk."

Whipping off her oversize sunglasses, she strode past Angela with the air of a runway model. Her perfume was strong, and her white business suit was so tight, it fit like a corset.

"I'm a very busy woman, with no time to waste, so I'm going to make this quick."

Angela snatched her silk robe off the floor and shrugged it back on. "What's going on?" she asked, closing the front door. "You're scaring me. Is Demetri okay?"

"Of course. Why wouldn't he be?" Her eyes roamed over Angela's body, moving slowly from top to bottom. "Demetri doesn't date fat girls, so I couldn't figure out how the hell you sunk your claws into him, but now that I know the truth about your past, it all makes sense. Sex-trade workers are the most manipulative people in the world."

Confused, Angela belted her robe. "I don't know what you're talking about."

"I bet you don't," she snapped, swiveling her neck. Her diamond, teardrop earrings tinkled like chimes. "You went to great lengths to hide your past, but I was smart enough to uncover the truth."

A cold chill snaked down Angela's back, and goose bumps seared her skin.

"I hired the best private investigator in the country, and he uncovered so much dirt on you, I could do my *own* three-part series." Nichola stared at her, her eyes blazing and her lips drawn tight. "And you know what I'd call my salacious exposé? *Newscaster for Hire*."

The floor fell out from underneath Angela's feet. Fear infected her entire body. She remained calm, but inside she was dying a slow, painful death. It felt as if her heart had been pierced with a knife. She was so overtaken by guilt and shame, water filled her eyes.

"I must admit, I was shocked when the P.I. told me the truth. You seem so polished, so sophisticated. I never would have guessed you were once a paid whore."

Angela winced and swallowed the lump wedged inside her

throat. This was a nightmare, the moment she had been dreading for years. Her heart pounded violently. No one knew—not her friends, not her family, not even Simone—that she'd worked as an escort to pay for university, and she had no intention of ever telling them. That was why she didn't do relationships, why she shied away from love.

"Don't tell Demetri," she pleaded. "Not now, not yet. He won't understand."

"Few men would. I mean, really, what guy wants to date a former prostitute?"

Angela felt a strong attack of guilt, but she looked straight at Nichola and spoke the truth. "I was never a prostitute. I was an escort. There's a big difference."

"No, there isn't. *Escort* is just a sophisticated word for *ho.* You screwed men for money, and from what the P.I. told me, you had a lot of fun doing it, too. In fact, you worked for Elite Escorts an entire year. That's a lot of sex and a lot of men, Angela."

"I never slept with any of my clients. Ever. Not one."

"Right, and that's your natural hair color!"

"It wasn't like that," Angela argued, refusing to back down. "My scholarship fell through, and I needed to make fast money. But after I paid my tuition, I quit."

"Cry me a river," she spat, twirling a finger in the air. "I heard that became-a-ho-to-pay-my-university-tuition story before."

"It's the truth."

"No, it's a crock of bull." Nichola rolled her eyes to the ceiling and swept a hand through her hair. "You became an escort because you're a whore, plain and simple."

"Leave," Angela said, pointing at the front door. Her head was throbbing, her nose was running, and she couldn't control the tremble in her voice. But Angela didn't care how she looked. All she cared about was getting rid of the publicist from hell. "Get out of my house and don't come back."

Nichola batted her eyelashes, wore an innocent face. "But we're not finished talking."

The cold, menacing look on Nichola's face shook Angela to the bone, but for the life of her she couldn't figure out what she'd done to warrant her wrath. "What have I ever done to you?" she asked, her confusion turning to anger. "Why are you doing this? Why are you trying to ruin my relationship with Demetri?"

"Because you don't deserve him."

"But you do?"

"Damn right I do! I've been by Demetri's side for the last twelve years, and thanks to me, he's one of the most popular athletes in the world." Nichola lifted her chin and threw her shoulders back. She looked pleased with herself, proud, as if she'd developed a cure for a deadly disease. "Things were going great until you came along. Now I hardly get to see him, and when I do, all he wants to talk about is how intelligent you are, how generous you are, how fun you are to be around. I'm sick of it!"

Her gaze was lethal, as cold as a trained assassin, and when she spoke her tone was shrill and bitter. "I have plans for me and Demetri, *big plans,* and I'm not going to let a two-bit whore who grew up in the hood steal my place. Got it?"

Angela lowered her eyes to the floor, stared intently at her stiletto-clad feet. She wished she had the power to just vanish into thin air. Listening to Nichola made her feel worthless, insignificant, and the more she insulted her, the smaller she felt. "What do you want from me?"

"I thought you'd never ask." Nichola broke out into a twisted smile. "Break up with Demetri tonight, or I'll tell him about your whoring past."

"You can't," she croaked, choking back a sob. Her eyes burned, heavy with tears. Angela willed herself to be strong, to keep it together, but when she imagined her life without Demetri in it, tears broke free and coursed furiously down her cheeks. The truth about her past would tear him apart, and the last thing Angela wanted to do was hurt him. Not after all the sweet, thoughtful things he'd done for her over the past three months. "Demetri can never find out about it."

"Fine, then do what I say and I'll keep my mouth shut."

"Can't we work something else out? I'll give you anything you want—"

"Don't you get it? All I want is Demetri. That's it." Nichola took her car keys out of her Hermès bag and slid her sunglasses back on. "Ta-ta. Gotta run. I'm meeting a producer from the network for drinks, and I can't afford to be late."

"Wait! Please! Can't we discuss this?"

Throwing open the front door, Nichola sashayed down the paved brick walkway wearing the brightest smile.

Seconds later, Nichola sped down the street in her red two-door coupe, her music blaring so loud, the windows in Angela's house shook. Unable to move, she slumped against the wooden railing, a sick, aching feeling in her heart.

Angela blinked back tears, pressing her eyes shut tight. The thick, warm air blew across her skin, but her body trembled uncontrollably. Her palms were damp, slick with perspiration, and her erratic heartbeat pounded in fear.

Albany Park was filled with the sounds of summer. Children shrieked and laughed as they jumped through sprinklers, cyclists zoomed up the sidewalk, and the ice-cream truck crawled down the street carrying the scent of milk chocolate. Angela didn't know how long she stood on her front porch, replaying Nichola's words in her head, but with each passing second, her feelings of despair and isolation grew.

It took supreme effort for Angela to turn around and walk inside the house. And when she saw the glass vase—the one Demetri had surprised her with last night—filled with a dazzling array of colored tulips, she broke down and started to cry again.

Dropping her face in her hands, she slumped against the

door and slid down to the cold hardwood floor. Grief consumed her, a sense of loss so profound, her heart throbbed in pain. Angela didn't have psychic powers, but as deep, racking sobs shook her body, she was certain of one thing: life as she knew it was over.

Chapter 19

Baseball fans in Chicago Royals jerseys and T-shirts were everywhere—on the sidewalk, standing on the hoods of their cars, waving frantically across the busy, traffic-congested street. And when Demetri strode out of Skyline Field, a cheer went up.

Angela had never seen anything like it. The crowd outside of the stadium seemed to be growing by the second, and everywhere she looked people were smiling and cheering. Teenage girls in tank tops and Daisy Dukes were crying, grown men where hollering Demetri's name, and a group of inebriated college kids were singing a slurred, off-key rendition of "Take Me Out to the Ball Game."

"Are you okay?" Demetri squeezed Angela's hand and sent her a reassuring smile.

"Yeah, I'm fine. Just a little overwhelmed, that's all."

He hit a button on his car keys, and the lights on his gleaming, white Jaguar flashed. The windows slid down, the sunroof opened, and the car stereo blared.

"Baby, get inside," he said, opening the passenger-side door. "People are pushing against the barricades, and I don't want you to get hurt."

Angela slid inside the car and watched as Demetri entertained the crowd. He signed posters, magazine covers and posed for dozens of pictures with his adoring fans. Twenty minutes after exiting the stadium, Demetri hopped into the front seat, threw it into Drive and shot down the block like a rocket.

"What's wrong?" Casting a glance at her, his facial expression filled with concern. He reached out and gently stroked the back of her neck.

"What makes you think something's wrong?"

"You're usually upbeat and chatty, but you haven't said more than a few words all day."

"I'm fine. I just have a lot on my mind."

"Want to talk about it?" His eyes twinkled when he smiled. "Go on, baby. I'm all ears."

His words made her feel a powerful rush of emotion. Tears burned the backs of her eyes. Willing herself not to cry, Angela ordered herself to be strong, to keep it together. It was the first time she'd seen Demetri all week, but instead of being excited about spending the entire day with him, she felt anxious and afraid. *Will this be the day Nichola tells Demetri about my past? Will he ever forgive me once he learns the truth?*

Angela thought about last Tuesday night, the day her life took a turn for the worst. After Nichola sashayed out of her house, Angela called Demetri and canceled their date. When he pressed her for an explanation, Angela told him she was sick. And she was. She had a queasy stomach and an excruciating headache that pulsed behind her right eye. A week later her symptoms remained.

"It's nothing." Angela tried to smile, to put his fears to rest, but her lips wouldn't curve upward. She couldn't summon the effort it took. Probably because she'd spent the past few days crying and stressing about the vicious threats Nichola had made. "I'm just tired," she lied, forcing a yawn. "A good night's rest and I'll be as good as new."

A shadow of disappointment fell across Demetri's face. They drove on in silence for several miles, and when he finally spoke, there was a note of sadness in his voice. "Didn't you enjoy the tour of the stadium and our picnic lunch?"

"Yes, of course. It was amazing. I loved every minute of it."

Demetri raised an eyebrow. "Are you sure?"

"I said I had a great time. Why don't you believe me?"

"Because you've been quiet and distant all afternoon, and every time I touch you, you tense up." He lowered his hand from her neck to her thigh, giving it a soft, playful squeeze. "Don't worry, baby. When we get home, I'll make everything better. A deep tissue massage will—"

"I can't stay with you tonight," Angela said, cutting him off. "I have to be at the station at five a.m., and I don't want to make that long drive back to my place in the morning."

"I know. That's why we're staying in the city tonight."

"You got a hotel room?"

"Just wait and see. We're almost there."

Angela turned toward the passenger-side window and pretended to admire all the tall, attractive buildings they sped by. Her mind replayed the afternoon. Strolling around the old, historic stadium, chatting with Demetri's teammates and sharing a romantic picnic lunch out on the field. It had been a memorable day, but it was hard staying upbeat when Nichola was texting her threatening messages. Angela thought about the last text message Nichola had sent, the one that caused her blood to run cold.

I wonder what would happen if the president of WJN-TV found out his hotshot new broadcaster used to be a call girl.

"I almost forgot. I have something for you."

Angela blinked and shook free of her thoughts. "Sorry, I missed that. What did you say?"

At the intersection, Demetri opened the center console and took out a thin, black blindfold. "I'll take it off as soon as we get to our mystery destination," he said with a wide smile. "And no peeking, baby. I want it to be a surprise."

Angela hated the thought of being blindfolded, but she didn't argue. A power nap would do her some good, and when Demetri tied the soft piece of cloth at the back of her head, her eyes grew heavy, and her muscles relaxed. As she snuggled down into her seat and curled up against the window, Angela felt the car jolt forward and then roll to a stop.

Ten minutes later, Angela was clutching Demetri's forearm and moving along the sleek tiled floor with short, measured steps. She heard an elevator ping, boisterous conversation around her, and the glare of bright overhead lights seeped in through the corner of her blindfold. Angela didn't know why she'd agreed to let Demetri blindfold her, but when she heard soft, romantic music playing, her trepidation waned and her interest peaked.

"Surprise! Welcome home!"

Demetri untied the blindfold, and when Angela saw the lavish suite decked out in marble and luxurious furniture, she recognized it immediately. They were in the penthouse suite at Trump International Hotel and Tower, their secret getaway in the heart of the city. The wall-length windows overlooking downtown Chicago provided a spectacular panoramic view, but Angela's favorite spot in the suite was the enclosed wraparound balcony.

Angela glanced around the suite, confused. The living room looked a lot like the one in her house. There were fashion magazines on the glass coffee table, a red velvet armchair, and a statue—just like the one she'd bought in Cancun—was sitting on the bookshelf. The teal walls weren't covered in expensive abstract paintings. Instead they were filled with dozens of framed candid pictures that Demetri had snapped on his cell phone when they were goofing around at his estate. Angela smiled when she thought about all the great times they'd had the past few months.

"What do you think? Do you love it?"

"Yeah, it's great. But why did you have the hotel redecorate the suite for one night?"

Demetri came up behind her and wrapped his hands around

her waist. "Not for one night. This is permanent, unless you want to redecorate again."

"I don't understand."

"This is our new place."

Angela stared at him, puzzled and confused by his words. "*Our* place?"

"I hate you making the drive to Lake County after dark, and since you don't like my driver picking you up after work, I decided to buy this penthouse." A proud grin stretched across his face. "Now you don't have to steal the designer bathrobes or pilfer the candy in the mini bar. Everything in here is yours for the taking!"

"This suite is amazing, and I appreciate the gesture, but we can't live together."

"Why not? We're practically living together now!" Demetri held her tight. "Angela, I love spoiling you and doing things to make you smile. Because of you, I have a new lease on life. For the first time in years, I feel as rejuvenated and healthy as I did my rookie year."

Angela shook her head and held her hands out in front of her. "This is all too much. The expensive gifts, the penthouse, this insane notion of us living happily ever after."

"What's so crazy about that?" Demetri turned her around to face him and cupped her chin softly in his hands. He pressed a gentle kiss to her forehead and spoke in a tender voice. "Baby, I'm committed to you, one hundred percent, all the way in. If I wasn't, I wouldn't be making future plans or taking you with me to Italy to meet my parents."

"Italy!" Angela shrieked, widening her eyes. "Please tell me you're joking."

"We're going Memorial Day weekend. And that's not all. We're staying at the…"

"Demetri, I can't go with you to Italy."

"Of course you can. You already booked the time off work, remember?"

"Yeah, so I can work on my next series, not to fly halfway around the world."

"You can work on the jet. It has everything you need. An office, a computer..."

"Demetri, I don't want to meet your parents."

His eyes darkened. "Why not?"

"Because I don't want them to read too much into our relationship. We're lovers, nothing more, and that's not going to change." The lie seared her lips and filled her mouth with such a bitter taste she couldn't swallow. Her stomach lurched, pitched violently to the right. "I told you from day one I wasn't looking for anything serious. We're having fun, lots of laughs and great sex. Don't make this out to be more than it is."

He gave her a blank look and rubbed his fingertips over his eyes. "Angela, what are you talking about? Where is all this coming from?"

A war was waging in her heart as Nichola's words tormented her troubled mind. An unseen force urged her to tell Demetri the truth about her past, but she couldn't make her lips form the words. Her eyes were teary, her throat was dry, and when Demetri sank onto the leather couch and raked his hands over his head, her heart broke in two. Angela loved Demetri with all her heart, more than she'd ever loved anyone before, and the days they had spent together were the happiest of her life. His kisses were magical, his touch made her feel sexy, and being in his arms was the best feeling in the world. It killed her to know that he was hurting and that she'd been the one to cause him pain, but Angela couldn't tell Demetri—or anyone else—that she used to be an escort.

"I'm not cut out for relationships—you know that," she said, adopting a playful tone. "I hate being tied down, and after a while, dating the same person gets boring. That's why I like to play the field, you know, keep my options wide open."

Demetri's head snapped up. Lines of confusion creased

his forehead. He was breathing so heavily, Angela couldn't hear the music from the stereo.

"You're dating other guys?" His tone was sharp, filled with anger and accusation. He stared at her with contempt in his eyes. "Who? How many?"

"Why does it matter? We're both free to date and *do* whoever we want."

He slammed his fists on the armrest and rose to his feet. For a long moment he studied her with a lethal expression. The veins in his neck were stretched so tight, Angela was scared they'd snap. The next words he spoke were through clenched teeth, in a tone she'd never heard him use before, one that made her feel empty inside. "I won't share you, Angela. Not now, not ever."

"That's not your decision to make."

"Then we're through."

Angela didn't know what possessed her to touch him, to reach out and rest a hand on his cheek, but she did. To her surprise, he didn't pull away. This was the last time they'd ever be this close, the last time she'd ever have Demetri all to herself, and the thought made it hard to breathe. Angela saw pain etched on his face, a heartbreaking sadness that tore her up inside.

"Look me in the eye," he ordered, gripping her shoulders, "and tell me you don't love me. Tell me the last three months meant absolutely nothing to you."

Angela opened her mouth but quickly closed it. She couldn't do it, couldn't lie.

"I'm not the right girl for you, Demetri. You deserve someone better, someone you can be proud to take home to your parents."

"Baby, what are you talking about? You're the most remarkable woman I've ever met," he praised. "You work your ass off down at the station but still find time to volunteer, mentor teenage girls and burn dinner for me at least once a week."

Angela smothered a laugh, but inside she was smiling. She was being a royal first-class jerk to Demetri, but here he was, complimenting her. For as long as she lived, she'd never forget him or the love they shared.

"I want you, Angela. Only you, and no one else."

"I'm sorry, Demetri, but I can't do this anymore. I need my space and the freedom to do what I want, whenever I want. You're a great guy, but I'm tired of feeling smothered."

"Smothered?"

"Yeah, smothered," she said, opening her purse and rummaging around inside for nothing. Her eyes were stinging, and Angela knew if she didn't leave soon, the tears would surely fall. "I better get out of here. I have a full day ahead of me tomorrow."

"Angela, you sure this is what you want?"

His voice was muffled, and for a second Angela feared that he was going to cry. He wouldn't, of course. He was Demetri Morretti, a superstar athlete who had beautiful women like Nichola Caruso at his disposal. Men like Demetri, young, handsome, ridiculously wealthy, didn't stay single for long, and Angela knew he'd have another girl on his arm by the end of the week. At least that was what she told herself when guilt troubled her conscience.

She leaned in and gave Demetri a peck on the cheek and forced a smile. "Have fun in Italy. And good luck this season."

Then Angela turned and walked away. She'd played her role to the hilt, but when she stepped onto the private elevator and the heavy steel doors closed, her facade cracked. Her vision blurred, and for a long, dizzying moment she couldn't breathe. Angela slapped away the tears as they spilled down her cheeks, but nothing could assuage the aching void in her heart.

Chapter 20

Angela opened the refrigerator, took out the plastic container filled with barbecue chicken wings and strode out the back door. The sky was free of clouds, the air was thick and humid, and a hot breeze blew through her. Her colorful, long dress whipped around her ankles as she ambled through the backyard.

Angela fanned a hand in front of her face. It was scorching outside, at least ninety degrees, but her dad didn't seem to mind the sweltering heat. He was standing beside the grill, singing in perfect pitch to the Motown classic playing on his battered stereo. Like the CD player, the grill looked as though it was on its last legs. Every few minutes, it conked out, and when her dad turned it back on, smoke billowed out the hood. *Tomorrow, I'm buying him a new one,* Angela decided, resting the container on the wooden picnic table. *And a new stereo, too!*

Within the hour, the backyard would be filled with family and friends looking to celebrate Memorial Day by cutting loose, getting down and eating finger-lickin'-good barbecue. Angela was looking forward to catching up with her relatives and playing a game or two of dominoes with her uncles. But every time she heard an airplane in the distance, she couldn't help but think about Demetri. This was the weekend they should have been in Italy, visiting his family and taking in the sights, but because of the things she'd said and done, they were over. Angela told herself it was for the best, that it was better being alone than living a lie, but if that was true, why did she feel as if she were going to die of a broken heart?

It had been a week since their breakup, and each day was harder than the one before. At work, Angela was the consummate professional, but at night, when she was alone, thoughts of Demetri and the love they'd shared consumed her. For hours, she'd lie in bed, staring up at the ceiling, lamenting over what could have been. These days she was such a basket case she considered seeking professional help. When she wasn't crying, she was on her laptop watching old Chicago Royals games and interviews.

Eye on Chicago was still number one with viewers, but ever since her interview with Demetri and his brothers had gone up in smoke, Salem had been giving her the cold shoulder. *Who cares?* Angela thought, raking a hand through her windswept hair. *The man I love hates me.*

Loud music filled the air, and when she heard a car door slam in the distance, she knew her brother had arrived. Rodney strode into the backyard carrying a case of beer in one hand and plastic bags filled with junk food in the other.

"Hey, sis, what's up?" Rodney asked, flashing a smile at her.

Angela had nothing to smile about, so she nodded her head instead. It was the first time she'd seen him since running into him at Madison's Steak Bar a few weeks back with Demetri. But he leaned over and dropped a kiss on her cheek anyway, as if everything were cool between them. It wasn't, but Angela knew better than to argue with Rodney in front of her dad.

"Here, this is for you." He pushed a wad of money, secured with a plastic elastic band, into her hands and winked. "Don't spend it all in one place."

Frowning, Angela glanced from the cash to her brother. "Where did you get this?"

"From work, of course!" Rodney rolled his eyes. "I got my

first paycheck today, and after taking out a grand for you, I still have a little left over in my savings to buy—"

"You have a savings account?" Shaking her head, Angela dropped down in the checkered lawn chair behind her. "Someone pinch me. I must be dreaming!"

"I told you your brother would get his act together." Cornelius wagged his plastic spatula at his daughter. "He just needed some time."

"And a break," he added, sending Angela a smile. "Thanks again for the hookup, sis. Working for the Royals is a real sweet gig."

"You're working at Skyline Field? How did that happen?"

"A couple days after I ran into you and Demetri at that posh restaurant, he called and told me the stadium was looking for new ushers. I wasn't interested *until* he told me the pay was twenty bucks an hour. Then I told him, 'Hell yeah!'"

"I had no idea he called you."

"Really, but Demetri said he was hiring me as a favor to you."

Angela shook her head. "I had nothing to do with you getting the job."

"For real? So, my charm and good looks got me the gig?" Rodney smiled wide. "I guess I'm just fly like that!"

Cornelius stroked his beard reflectively. "Maybe I was wrong about Demetri Morretti. Maybe he isn't as bad as I thought."

"Pops, Demetri's mad cool," Rodney said, his tone full of admiration. "He's real laid-back, and everyone down at the field loves him."

"Is that right?"

"Demetri knows everyone by name—even the janitors—and he's the best tipper on the team. Yesterday, he gave me a hundred bucks just for vacuuming his Bentley!"

"That's hard to believe." Cornelius opened the cooler, took

out a can of Pepsi and broke the tab. "I read that he's a trou-blemaker, a real hothead."

"Now that I've gotten to know him, I don't believe the hype anymore."

Cornelius grinned. "Rodney, you don't know Demetri Morretti any more than I do. You've only been working there a couple weeks."

"Yeah, but I've seen firsthand all the crap Demetri and his teammates go through."

"Please." Cornelius dismissed his son's words with a flick of his hand. "They live in million-dollar homes, drive flashy sports cars and can afford to buy the very best of everything. What's so hard about that?"

"I used to envy pro athletes, but now that I know what goes on behind the scenes, I actually feel sorry for them," Rod-ney said. "People are always trying to provoke Demetri into fights so they can cash in on his money. Everyone wants fif-teen minutes of fame, and they'll do just about anything to get it, including…"

Angela sat up, listening with rapt interest as Rodney spoke. What he said was true, every single word. She'd seen first-hand how cruel society could be to celebrities. Whenever she was out with Demetri, he was constantly looking over his shoulder. He craved privacy and didn't want to be sur-rounded by the paparazzi. But to make her happy he'd taken her to festivals, shows and anywhere else her heart desired.

"Demetri said if I work hard and have the right attitude, the team might even pay for me to go to trade school. Isn't that crazy?"

"You want to go to trade school? Since when?"

Rodney shrugged. "I'm just thinking about it. Demetri thinks I'm smart, and he said if I apply myself, I could make something of myself…"

Angela slid farther down her lawn chair. She tried to man-age her emotions the best she could, but it was hard to keep her composure when all she wanted to do was cry. Being without Demetri was killing her, and hearing Rodney talk about what a great guy he was only intensified her guilt. Her brother was spot-on, though. Demetri was an amazing man, hands down the sweetest, most generous person she'd ever met.

"Demetri doesn't sound half-bad," Cornelius said, slowly nodding his head. "Now I see why you and Angela like him so much."

Not like, Dad, love. I love him with all my heart.

Her gaze fell on her cell phone, which was sitting on the pile of board games. Angela wanted to call Demetri to apologize for the way she'd acted last week and thank him for helping Rodney, but she was too afraid. What if Nichola had told him about her past?

The sun was still strong, making Angela unbearably hot, yet her entire body was shaking. Her past was hanging over her head, tormenting her day and night. The dirty little secret she'd been keeping for years had prevented her from falling in love and giving herself completely to any man, and Angela was tired. Tired of running from her past and the man she loved. She'd let fear stop her from telling Demetri the truth, but she knew if she didn't come clean to the people she loved, she'd never be able to move forward.

"Did you invite Demetri and his people to come over today?"

Angela glanced up at her dad and shook her head.

"Why not? I'd love to meet him."

"It's not going to happen, Dad. We're through."

Her father's jaw dropped, and Rodney groaned.

"Baby girl, what happened?" Cornelius put his soda can down on the wooden picnic table. He plopped down in the chair beside her and took her hand. "You've been talking my ear off for weeks about how great Demetri is. I thought you really liked him."

I love him, Dad, more than I've ever loved anyone before.

"It's a long, sad story. One you definitely don't want to hear."

"Of course I do. I'm your dad, and anything that affects you affects me."

"But I did something *really* stupid. Something I'm deeply ashamed of."

Cornelius hugged her to his chest and dropped a kiss on her forehead. "Everyone makes mistakes, Angela, and there's nothing you could ever say that would make me love you any less."

"Same here, sis. You're my shero!" Rodney's eyes were watery, but he wore a big, goofy grin. "Now, stop crying. We're having a party this afternoon, remember?"

Angela didn't realize she was crying until her dad grabbed a napkin off the picnic table and wiped her cheeks. His slim, narrow face was pinched with concern. The setting was all wrong, and so was the timing, but Angela knew if she didn't tell her dad the truth now, she'd never do it. So, she swallowed the knot in her throat and gave his hand a light squeeze. "Dad, can we go inside and talk?" she asked, ignoring the butterflies flittering around in her stomach. "There's something I have to tell you. Something I should have told you years ago."

Chapter 21

Demetri stepped up to the plate and tried a few practice swings. His right arm felt strong, better than it had in months. *How fitting,* he thought, shaking his head. *The same week I'm cleared to practice with the team my relationship with Angela goes up in smoke.*

Tired of lifting weights in his gym, he'd headed outside to his enclosed seven-foot batting cage, determined. The air was still and held the faint scent of rain. It was the first time Demetri had been outside all week, and the sun was so bright, it irritated his eyes.

Tucking his baseball bat under his arm, he took his shades out of his back pocket and slid them on. Now he could focus. Or at least pretend to. These days, he thought about Angela, and nothing else. He had been so bummed about their breakup, he didn't have the strength to leave the house. It was easier to stay home than deal with the world. For the past week, he'd done nothing but eat, sleep and relive every second of his last conversation with Angela. And, still, after all this time, he couldn't make sense of what went wrong.

The machine spit out a fast ball, and Demetri swung the wooden baseball bat with such force, he felt a slight twinge in his right shoulder. It was probably nothing, but he made a mental note to speak to his surgeon about it tomorrow at his checkup.

For the next hour, Demetri took his frustration and anger out on the pitches. And by the time he was finished practicing, his blue Nike T-shirt was drenched in sweat.

"Lookin' good, bro! You'll be back on the mound in no time!"

Demetri looked up and saw Nicco and Rafael leaning against the metal chain-link fence and gave them a nod. "What's up? I had no idea you guys were coming to town."

Rafael gave a shrug of his shoulder. "It was a last-minute decision."

"How was Argentina?"

"Sinful," Nicco said with a straight face. "But I loved every minute of it."

"I bet you did." Demetri narrowed his eyes and zeroed in on his brother's left forearm. The words *Dolce Vita* were tattooed in block letters down the length of his arm. "I see you got some new ink while you were in Buenos Aires."

"It hurt like a bitch, but the female tattoo artist gave me *exceptional* care afterwards."

"That's why you skipped my cricket match? Because you were too busy hooking up with some random chick?" Rafael looked relaxed in his striped polo shirt and khaki shorts, but when he glared at Nicco, his entire disposition changed. "Do you have to bed every woman you meet?"

"Of course not." Nicco wore a sly smile. "Only the sexy ones, bro. You know that."

Demetri and Rafael shook their heads.

"Speaking of chicks, are you still bangin' that smokin'-hot TV newscaster?"

Demetri's jaw tightened. "Her name is Angela."

"My bad." Nicco chuckled, held up a hand in a gesture of peace. "You still hittin' that?"

"Knock it off, Nicco. I'm not in the mood."

"You got too clingy, and she dumped you, huh?" Releasing a heavy sigh, he stepped inside the batting cage and clapped Demetri on the shoulder. "When are you going to learn that love doesn't last? Guys like us aren't cut out for relationships.

We're players, lady-killers, men who live for the thrill of the chase. That's just who we are, Demetri. It's in our blood."

Rafael scratched his head and then gave it a hard shake. "Nicco, what are you talking about? It's not in our blood to mistreat women or dog them out. Mom and Dad have been happily married for almost forty years, and he still dotes on her!"

"Yeah, but Moms is old-school. They don't make 'em like her anymore. If they did, I would have burned my player card a long time ago!"

"Nicco's right. Modern women are out for themselves," Rafael conceded with a shrug. "I went out with that cute boutique buyer again last week, and after dessert, she gave me her bank-account number and told me to deposit her weekly allowance in a timely manner."

"At least she didn't steal your Benz and hightail it down to Tijuana!" A scowl wrinkled Nicco's tanned face. "All women do is take, take, take."

Demetri heard the edge in Nicco's tone and sympathized with him. Unfortunately, he knew exactly what his brother was talking about. From the day he'd turned pro, he'd seen how ugly and manipulative people could be. He didn't trust easily and had always believed that everyone outside of his inner circle was out to screw him over.

But then he'd met Angela.

Over time, she'd changed his views about the world. She didn't care about his wealth or his fame, or spending his money, either. Angela loved him—just him—and she wasn't afraid to check him when he was wrong. His girl told him what he needed to hear, not what he *wanted* to hear, and Demetri respected her for always telling the truth. "Angela's never asked me for a dime," he said. "Hell, she wouldn't even let me take her shopping, and every time we went out for dinner, she insisted on leaving a tip *on top* of my tip!"

The brothers chuckled.

"I'm never settling down," Nicco announced, raking a hand through his short, curly black hair. "I'll be a player until I die!"

"Not if Mom can help it," Rafael said. "She wants daughters-in-law and grandbabies, and she's not beneath plotting and scheming to get them, either!"

"Forget about Angela Kelly and move on to the next chick."

"That's just it, Nicco. I can't," Demetri confessed, staring out into the bright blue sky. Being in a loving, committed relationship was who he was, who he'd always been. He wanted Angela—and no one else.

"The best way to get over a girl is by banging a new one." Nicco grinned. "That *always* works for me."

"If I can't have Angela, then I don't want anyone."

Two weeks had passed since Angela walked out on him. He thought of her day and night and would look at the pictures of her on his cell phone for hours. Demetri had racked his brain trying to piece together why she'd lashed out at him. But he'd come to only one conclusion and that was that Angela had lied to him. She wasn't dating other guys, wasn't seeing anyone else. When she wasn't at work, she was with him, and on the few occasions she went out with her girlfriends, she texted him throughout the night. So, why would she make up a story about sleeping with other guys? Why would she intentionally try to hurt him?

"If I were you, I'd…" Nicco broke off speaking and whipped out his cell phone. "Hold up, guys. I need to take this call."

"Something Angela said at the penthouse has been bothering me for weeks," Demetri said aloud. "She said I deserve someone better, someone I could be proud to take home to my family. At the time, I didn't think too much of it, but now it keeps playing in my mind."

"It sounds like your girl's running scared."

"Of what?"

Rafael gave a shrug. "You won't know unless you talk to her."

"I can't."

"Why not?"

"Because she doesn't want me. She wants to play the field." Inwardly, Demetri winced, but outwardly he wore a hard, stern face. He had to. He couldn't let anyone know—not even his brothers—how much he was hurting. The truth was, he missed Angela so much, his body ached with need. He yearned to hear her voice, to feel her touch, to have her unconditional love, and he wondered how he could ever live without her.

"Son of a bitch!" Nicco shouted, kicking the metal chain-link fence.

"What's the matter?"

"My assistant quit and is threatening to sue."

Rafael narrowed his eyes and wore a disgusted face. "You slept with her, didn't you?"

"It was an innocent mistake." Nicco dragged a hand down the length of his face and released a deep sigh. "I had too much to drink one night, and one thing led to another…"

"You're unbelievable," Rafael fumed, folding his arms rigidly across his chest. "It's time to grow up, Nicco. You're not a kid anymore, and I'm sick of fixing your mistakes."

Nicco started to speak but stopped when his cell phone rang again. He put it to his ear and turned away from his brothers. He spoke soft Italian to the caller on the line.

"I've only met Angela once, but it's obvious she makes you happy," Rafael said, his scowl gone and his smile sincere. "Since you guys started dating, you've become more outgoing, and now you're using your celebrity status for good. That's great, bro."

"The woman called me out on national television! I had to get my act together, *fast*."

"Demetri, don't let pride or your fear of rejection keep you from the woman you love." Rafael blew out a deep breath. "I did that once and to this day I regret not fighting for her. If Angela's the one, don't let anything get between you."

Demetri pondered his brother's words, truly considering what he'd said, and realized that Rafael was right. He had to fight for Angela, had to do whatever it took to get her back. She was his world and he wanted to spend the rest of his life with her. He was ready to go the distance, ready to make her his lawfully wedded wife. He wanted kids, family trips and the whole nine yards.

"Thanks, bro. You're the best!" Demetri chucked his baseball bat to the ground, kissed his brother on both cheeks and ran out of the batting cage. "Gotta jet. See you guys later!"

Chapter 22

Demetri jogged past the greenhouse and raced through the patio doors as if his life depended on it. And it did. He had to get to his girl, had to see her right away. He refused to live another day without her. Demetri was so consumed with thoughts of reconciling with Angela, he bumped into Nichola as she stepped out of the kitchen pantry.

"Where's the fire?" she joked, dumping the bags of potato chips on the granite breakfast bar. "Do you and your brothers want to eat lunch outside on the patio or in the game room?"

"I'm not staying. I'm going to see Angela."

"You two broke up."

"I'll explain later." Demetri glanced around the kitchen and saw all of the food trays and bottles of wine artfully arranged on the glass table. "It looks great in here."

"I made all your favorites and a whole pitcher of that sangria punch you love so much."

"Thanks, Nichola," he said, patting her shoulder. "Ask the housekeepers to clean the master suite and to fill all the vases in the living room with yellow tulips. I'm bringing my baby back home tonight, and I want everything to be perfect!"

"Hell no! That bitch isn't welcome here."

Demetri felt his nostrils flare and his hands curl into fists. "Excuse me?"

"If you bring Angela here, I'm leaving."

"Okay. See you tomorrow."

"I'm serious, Demetri. I'll walk out that door, and I won't

come back." Nichola puffed out her cheeks. "You don't need Angela or anyone else. All you need is me."

"Nichola, it's obvious you've had too much to drink," Demetri said, trying to lighten the mood with a joke. "Go home and sleep it off, and we'll talk in the morning."

"But I have good news. That's why I'm here. We're celebrating!" She rushed over to the glass table, picked up two cocktail glasses and pushed one into his hand. "Your new reality show, *Demetri's Bachelor Pad,* starts filming in September!"

Demetri scratched his head. He'd been out of sorts all week, and as grumpy as an old bear, but he didn't remember Nichola ever mentioning a TV deal. "I don't want my own show, Nichola. I'm a baseball player, not a reality star."

"But the network is rolling out the red carpet for you." Nichola was so excited, she was practically shouting her words. "Since I came up with the concept for the series *and* developed a kick-ass marketing campaign, they've agreed to let me be executive producer of the show!"

"Still not interested," he said. "And I don't care how much they're paying."

"Why not? This show could open a lot of doors for you."

"I'm a private person. I'd hate the idea of cameras following me and Angela around twenty-four seven. It's creepy. I won't do it."

Nichola held up an index finger. "Would you stop talking about her for one second and give some serious thought about this million-dollar deal?"

"There's nothing to think about. My priorities are baseball, my family, Angela and—"

"Forget about that skank. She's a whore and you deserve better."

Demetri narrowed his eyes. The more he stared at his publicist, the more convinced he was that she was drunk. Her skin was pale, and her face possessed a crazed expression. It took supreme effort to control his temper, but he spoke in a calm, rational voice. "Don't ever talk about Angela like that again," he warned. "I don't know what your problem is with her, but I'm not going to let you disrespect her."

"I called her a skank because that's what she is." A smile filled her lips, and her eyes lit up like diamonds. "Your precious Angela used to be an escort."

Demetri heard what Nichola had said, but he didn't understand. He stood paralyzed as her words turned over in his mind. He didn't believe it. His publicist was lying, just trying to poison his mind. *But why?*

"I hired a private investigator to check her out, and he uncovered a ton of dirt about her."

"You did what?" The question exploded out of Demetri's mouth. "For what reason? I never asked you to."

"Thank God I did, or you would have done something stupid like marry her!"

"Nichola, watch yourself," he warned. "You're out of line."

"You know what else the P.I. told me?"

Her nose wrinkled in disgust, but the expression on her face was one of pure joy. Nichola was enjoying every minute of this. For some sick reason she took great pleasure in smashing his hopes and dreams for the future.

"Angela's mother died five years ago from a drug overdose. Shoot, for all you know, she could be a druggie like her crackhead mom."

"Dammit, Nichola. Stop!"

Closing his eyes didn't block out the loud, shrill noises in his head. He heard Angela's tearful voice, then Nichola's harsh biting tone, playing in his mind over and over again. *You don't deserve someone like me. You deserve better.... Forget about her, Demetri.... She's a whore and you deserve better....* He was puzzled for a second, surprised that both women had virtually told him the exact same thing, but then something clicked. Everything made sense.

Demetri's eyes shot open. Stepping forward, he asked Nichola the question circling his mind. "You confronted Angela about what the private investigator told you, didn't you?"

"Of course I did. It's my job. That's what any good publicist would do."

"You told her she wasn't good enough for me, that I deserve better?"

"Why does it matter? She's gone, so forget her and move on." Her tone was firm, all business, as if she were chairing a board meeting. And she looked the part, too, standing there in a fitted black dress and wearing millions in diamonds. "It's time to move on to bigger and better things, like your *own* show."

Anger burned in Demetri's veins. He was so enraged that he wanted to grab Nichola and shake some sense into her. But instead of going after his publicist, he paced the length of the room. Three months ago, he would have punched a hole in the wall. But he wasn't the same man he used to be. He'd matured. He'd learned to see the world through Angela's eyes. And he wasn't going to embarrass his family or the woman he loved ever again. "I can't deal with this right now," he said, dragging a hand down the length of his face. "I need some time to think."

"What's there to think about? I know what's best for you, and it's this opportunity."

"I'm not talking about the reality show. I'm talking about Angela."

"God," she raged, throwing her hands up in the air. "I'm sick of hearing her stupid name! Enough already! I got rid of her, and she's not coming back, so…"

Her tone consumed Demetri with such rage he couldn't see straight. It broke his heart to think that Angela was hurting and that Nichola—someone he trusted—was the cause. He wanted to hate her, but his heart wouldn't let him. Nichola had been his publicist for twelve long years, and he loved her like a sister. But that didn't mean he was going to forgive and forget what she'd done. Her behavior was hard to justify and impossible to condone. Demetri pointed at the front door. "Nichola, you're fired. Please leave."

Her smile vanished. "Y-y-you can't fire me."

"I'll have my accountant put your final check and an official letter of termination in the mail first thing tomorrow."

Nichola stared at him in horror, as if she'd just seen a ghost.

His heart was heavy, filled with frustration and disappointment. He was so disgusted by Nichola's behavior, he couldn't stand to be in the same room with her a moment longer. "I want you gone by the time I finish getting dressed."

"Demetri, don't do this," she begged. "I love you. I've always loved you."

"You don't love me. You love the benefits of managing a celebrity."

"Of course I do. Who wouldn't?" Nichola's smile was back, shining in full force. "With my brains and beauty and your talent, we could be the next celebrity power couple."

Demetri didn't bother to answer. Shaking his head, he turned toward the staircase.

Nichola grabbed his forearm and threw herself against him. "Come back!"

Breaking free of her grasp, Demetri strode out of the room and down the hallway. He heard glass break, then an ear-splitting wail, but he continued upstairs to the second floor.

In the master bedroom, Demetri fell down on the bed and dropped his head into his hands. *Angela used to be an escort...an escort...* The word froze in his brain. Demetri didn't know what to think, didn't know what to believe. He wanted to make sense of what Nichola had said. What if it was true? What if Angela used to be an escort?

So what? his inner voice said. *Everyone has a past, even you.*

The truth slammed into him with the force of a battering ram. He'd made a lot of mistakes in the past and had done things he was ashamed of, but things had changed for the better when he'd met Angela Kelly—the strong, tenacious TV newscaster who lived to help others. It didn't matter what Angela had done in her past. All that mattered to him was the here and now.

He wasn't going to shut her out or lump her in with all the other lying, conniving women he'd had the misfortune of meeting in the past. He'd known from the first time they'd met that Angela was different. She challenged him, inspired him and wasn't afraid to speak her mind. They had great talks about life, their families and the stress of being famous in a celebrity-obsessed world. Angela cared about, loved him despite his faults and shortcomings and put his needs above her own. Finally, Demetri understood why she'd lied to him that night in the penthouse suite. It wasn't because she didn't love him, but because she *did*.

Demetri rose to his feet and headed into his walk-in closet. Kicking off his sneakers, he searched through his dress shirts for something to wear. "Call Angela at home," he said aloud. The cordless phone dialed the number, and after three rings, her voice mail picked up. Her sweet, sultry voice filled the room, and thoughts of loving her consumed him. "Baby, it's me. Call me back. We need to talk," he said after hearing the phone beep.

Demetri tried her cell phone next, and when she picked up on the first ring, he charged over to the dresser and snatched the cordless phone off the base. "Angela?"

"Hey," she said, her tone somber.

His shoulders caved, and his heart fell. He heard the apprehension in her voice and wondered how things had gotten so bad, so fast between them. "I need to see you. We have to talk."

"I can't. Now's not a good time."

"It's important that I see you as soon as possible."

"Why? What else is there to say?"

Demetri heard a loud, piercing scream and stared down at the phone.

"What was that?"

"I'm at the hospital."

"Why? What happened? Are you okay?"

"I'm good, but I can't say the same for Simone. Her water broke while we were having lunch at the Skyline Grill."

"How's Marcus doing?"

"Great," she said with a laugh. "His daughters aren't even born yet, but he's already handing out Cuban cigars!"

He loved to hear Angela laugh. He didn't want to ruin her mood, but he had to know the truth. He opened his mouth, prepared to ask her about the accusations Nichola had made, but the question died on his lips. This was the wrong time. More than anything, he needed to hold her in his arms. "I miss you, baby. I miss us."

"I do, too, Demetri, but things are confusing right now. I just need some time."

"Come to the estate after you leave the hospital."

"I don't know if I can…"

"Please?" he begged, not caring how desperate he sounded. He *was* desperate—desperate to touch her, to kiss her, to stroke her soft, smooth cheeks and her flawless brown skin. "If you don't come to me, then I'll just have to come to you."

"No!" Her tone was sharp enough to cut glass. "We can't do this today, not here, not now. I promised Simone I'd be in the delivery room for the birth of her daughters, and I'm not going to let her down. We'll just have to get together another time."

Demetri thought hard, racking his brain for the right words to say. He had to say something, had to prove to Angela once and for all that he loved her—unconditionally. "Let's meet at the penthouse to talk. I'm headed there now."

"I don't know."

"Come on, baby. You can do better than that. Say yes."

Every second that ticked by worried Demetri more. "I just want to talk. That's it."

Dead silence settled over the line.

"Okay, I'll be there."

Demetri released the breath he was holding and smiled for the first time all day. "Hurry, baby. I'll be waiting."

Chapter 23

"Good morning," the robust security guard said from his perch in front of the reception area. "Welcome to WJN-TV, home of five Emmy Award–winning shows."

Demetri couldn't believe his good fortune. The security guard, who'd taken him to Angela's studio that fateful morning three months ago, was on duty. *Finally, something's going my way,* he thought, pausing in front of the bronze statue to check his cell phone. There had been no missed calls or text messages. No word from Angela whatsoever. She hadn't turned up at the penthouse suite on Monday night, and if not for Nicco threatening to disown him, he would have stormed Mercy Hospital looking for her. But that morning, after waking from a restless night of sleep, he'd decided enough was enough. He had to see Angela today. No matter what. And he'd driven to WJN-TV at the first light of day. He had to talk to her face-to-face.

As Demetri strode past the elevators, a hush fell over the lobby. He heard people whispering, saw cameras flash, felt the heat of a dozen wide-eyed stares. Hearing his cell phone buzz, he stared down at the screen.

His muscles tensed as he furiously clutched his phone. For the past three days, Nichola had been blowing up his phone, but he hadn't answered any of her calls. He didn't want to talk to her. At least not yet. Once he worked things out with Angela, he'd hash things out with his former publicist—but not a moment sooner. "What's up?" Demetri said, approaching his favorite security guard. "It's good to see you again, man."

The smile slid off the guard's wide, fleshy face. "What do you want?" Anger clouded his eyes and crimped his lips. "Because of the stunt you pulled the last time you were here, I got written up, and my hours were cut."

"My bad, man. I didn't mean to get you in trouble."

"You insulted a newscaster! What did you *think* was going to happen?"

Demetri noticed the security guard's name tag and then lowered his eyes to the floor, as if he were consumed with shame. "I feel terrible."

"You should. Everyone's not a millionaire like you." His voice was heavy with sarcasm. "I need this job to support my family."

Demetri reached into his back pocket, removed a small white envelope and offered it to the security guard. "Jorge, this is for you. I want you and three of your friends to be my guests at the celebrity baseball game next month."

His tongue lay limp in his open mouth. "Y-y-you do?"

"Of course. You're my number one fan, right?"

The security guard snatched the envelope out of Demetri's hand. "These are box seats! Box seats!" he chirped, waving the tickets in the air. "Those seats are worth five grand apiece."

Demetri clapped the security guard on the shoulder and motioned toward the corridor with his head. "I need you to take me to Angela's studio one last time."

The security guard shook his head. "I can't. Company rules. Unauthorized visitors aren't allowed in Studio A anymore. Not even celebrity ones."

"I'm not here to make trouble."

"But the last time you were here—"

Demetri cut him off. "The last time I was here I was trippin' big-time, but I'm not here to upset Angela."

"I don't know about this." Sweat broke out across his fore-head and drenched the front of his navy blue shirt. "I can't afford to lose this job. My old lady will kill me."

"She'll be happy to see me, Jorge. I know it."

"You're sure?"

"Positive." Demetri forced a smug look. The truth was, he didn't know what to believe anymore, but if he wavered, even for a second, the security guard would toss him out. And noth-ing was more important to Demetri than seeing Angela. He had to trust his gut. Something told him they were going to make it, that they'd be okay. "We've been dating for months. Haven't you heard?"

"I heard this morning on the radio that she dumped you."

"It was one big misunderstanding. That's why I'm here. To apologize."

Jorge wore a small smile and nodded as if he understood. He spoke quietly to the receptionist, and after several minutes of heated conversation, the frizzy-haired blonde buzzed open the door to her left. As Jorge led Demetri down the corridor, he jawed about the celebrity baseball game and fretted over whom he should bring to the event.

Outside Studio A, Demetri put a hand on Jorge's shoulder and gave him a stern look. "Turn off your cell phone, Jorge."

"My phone? What phone? I, ah, left it in my truck."

"The last time I was here, you recorded my conversation with Angela and posted it online. Not cool at all," he said. "I don't like being the butt of people's jokes."

"It wasn't me. I swear."

"Don't play me." Demetri glared at Jorge to let him know he meant business. "I could tell by the angle the video was shot. You were standing right here, just inside the door, film-ing your little heart out."

Jorge shuffled his feet and fiddled with the walkie-talkie in his pocket. "I recorded the video just for kicks, but I wasn't the one who posted it online. I sent it to a couple friends, and the next thing I know it was on the six-o'clock news! Sorry, man. I didn't mean for it to get out."

"No screwups this time, okay? My entire future is riding on the next ten minutes."

"I won't let you down, Demetri. I promise." Jorge straightened his hunched shoulders and gave a salute. "What do you want me to do?"

"Just stand here and keep watch over this door," he said, gripping the shiny gold doorknob. "Make sure no one comes in. Think you can do that for me?"

"Of course. That's what they pay me for." Jorge chuckled. "Go get your girl, Demetri. Good luck!"

"Thanks, man. I have a feeling I'm going to need it."

"I want to do it all. Act, sing, dance, model," announced the bubbly tween star with the pink braces and glittery eye makeup. "I want to be the next big thing and nothing's going to stop me!"

Angela wanted to roll her eyes but smiled at the pop star instead. The twelve-year-old girl went on and on, jumping from one topic to the next. It was virtually impossible to stay focused, and when she broke out in song, Angela's mind wandered. Out of the corner of her eye, she studied the large wall clock at the back of the studio. *Ten more minutes and I'm out of here!*

"I'd love to come back on your show when my album drops this fall. It's called *Celebrity Love* and…"

Angela nodded, keeping her smile fixed in place. She needed to move the segment along, but she couldn't get a word in. Not one. Instead she sat there rehearsing what she wanted to say to Demetri when she arrived at his estate later that afternoon. Now that her family knew the truth, she could finally come clean to Demetri.

To ward off the tears stinging the backs of her eyes, Angela bit the inside of her cheek. Witnessing the birth of her twin goddaughters, Victoria and Aaliyah, had been a life-changing experience, and seeing how happy and close Simone and Marcus were made Angela hanker for a rock-solid marriage, too. She wanted babies—Demetri's babies—and the thought of spending the rest of her life with the man she loved, who completed her in every way, made Angela's heart swell with unspeakable joy.

A bright light suddenly flooded the studio, and a cold gush of air whipped through the room. Shivering, she crossed her legs and clasped her hands around her knees. Angela opened her mouth, a question poised on the tip of her tongue, but when she saw Demetri striding into the studio through one of the side doors, her mind went blank. Empty. Angela was so shocked, so stunned to see him, she convinced herself he was just a figment of her imagination.

Angela blinked, told herself to snap out of it. She had to be dreaming, fantasizing. No way Demetri was on her set, live and in the flesh—again. Only this time around he wasn't shooting evil daggers her way. He smelled dreamy, and if his smile was any bigger it could eclipse the sun. Angela expected security or her producer to stop him as he strode onto the set, but no one moved a muscle. She wanted to tell him that they were on live, but Angela couldn't get her mouth to work.

"I knew the first time I saw you, here on this very set, that you were the only woman for me." His voice was soft, as tender as a kiss along the curve of her spine. "I never dreamed that three months later I'd be madly in love with you, but I am. I love you with all my heart, with all that I am, and I want to spend the rest of my life with you."

Angela cupped a hand over her mouth to trap a scream inside. Her eyes filled with tears. Angela felt her heart pounding in her ears like a mighty rushing wind.

Demetri took her hands and helped her to her feet. Her palms, like her legs, were drenched in sweat and shaking uncontrollably. His gaze was intense, but the smile on his lips was comforting. His eyes glistened with amusement, making her feel light-headed and weak.

One of the station's interns marched onto the set carrying a silver tray. Wearing her brightest smile, she looked straight into the camera and whipped off the cover with a dramatic flourish. A velvet ring box sat on a bed of red rose petals. The fragrant scent filled the studio.

"I love everything about you. Your infectious smile, your upbeat attitude, the way you burn my breakfast just right." A grin crossed his lips when he winked. "I want to cook for you and laugh with you and watch *Family Feud* every morning with you in bed."

His words made her heart melt to a puddle at her feet. But Angela knew if they were going to have a future together, she had to tell Demetri the truth about her past. "There are things about me you don't know," she began, unable to hide the quiver in her voice. "Things that could affect our relationship and our future."

"Angela, there is absolutely nothing—" he reached out to her and cupped her chin "—you could say that will change how I feel about you. I believe in us, and I won't let anything or anyone come between us again."

The crew oohed and aahed.

"You're so beautiful, so perfect for me in every way," he praised, leaning forward and brushing his nose against her cheek. "You were made to be cherished, and I vow to love, honor and adore you for the rest of our lives."

A tear broke free and trickled down Angela's cheek.

"I want you to know and believe that." He rested a hand on her chest, and Angela covered it with her own. "You brought love and laughter back into my life, and for the first time in years, I'm genuinely happy. And it's all because of you."

Without looking, Demetri snatched the velvet ring box off of the tray and dropped to one knee. The cameraman wheeled the camera forward.